GREED

7 Deadly Sins Vol. 3

First published as a collection August 2018

Content copyright © Pure Slush Books and individual authors
Edited by Matt Potter

All rights reserved by the authors and publisher. Except for brief excerpts used for review or scholarly purposes, no part of this book may be reproduced in any manner whatsoever without express written consent of the publisher or the author/s.

Pure Slush Books
32 Meredith Street
Sefton Park SA 5083
Australia

Email: edpureslush@live.com.au
Website: https://pureslush.com/
Store: https://pureslush.com/store/

Original floating money image copyright © Quince Media
Cover design copyright © Matt Potter

ISBN: 978-1-925536-64-5

Also available as an eBook
ISBN: 978-1-925536-65-2

A note on differences in punctuation and spelling

Pure Slush Books proudly features writers from all over the English-speaking world. Some speak and write English as their first language, while for others, it's their second or third or even fourth language. Naturally, across all versions of English, there are differences in punctuation and spelling, and even in meaning. These differences are reflected in the work *Pure Slush Books* publishes, and they account for any differences in punctuation, spelling and meaning found within these pages.

Pure Slush Books is a member of the
Bequem Publishing collective
http://www.bequempublishing.com/

• Alex Reece ABBOTT • Meryl BAER • Alan C. BAIRD • Gary BECK • Paul BECKMAN • Jim BELL • Dennis Wayne BRESSACK • Howard BROWN • Michael H. BROWNSTEIN • Irene BUCKLER • Elizabeth BUTTIMER • Steven CARR • Guilie CASTILLO ORIARD • Chuka Susan CHESNEY • Jan CHRONISTER • Linda M. CRATE • Judah Eli CRICELLI • Tony DALY • Jo DAVIES • Salvatore DiFALCO • William DORESKI • Morgan DRISCOLL • Michael ESTABROOK • Claire FEILD • Alison FISH • Nod GHOSH • Ken GOSSE • Andrew GRENFELL • Shane GUTHRIE • Sharron HOUGH • Mark HUDSON • Abha IYENGAR • Christine JOHNSON • Jemshed KHAN • Andrei KONCHALOVSY • John LAMBREMONT Sr. • Ron LAVALETTE • Larry LEFKOWITZ • Cynthia LESLIE-BOLE • Mike LEWIS-BECK • Peter LINGARD • JP LUNDSTROM • DS MAOLALAI • Bryon McWILLIAMS • Barbara A. MEIER • Karla Linn MERRIFIELD • Ted MICO • Joe MILLS • Marsha MITTMAN • Piet NIEUWLAND • Edward O'DWYER • Carl 'Papa' PALMER • M PAUSEMAN • Martin Jon PORTER • Melisa QUIGLEY • David RAE • Niles REDDICK • Edward REILLY • Lisa RHODES-RYABCHICH • Copper ROSE • Ruth Sabath ROSENTHAL • Shawn Aveningo SANDERS • Robert SCOTELLARO • Wayne SCHEER • Jonathan SLUSHER • Caroline SMADJA • Lisa STICE • Foster TRECOST • Linda TYLER • Lucy TYRRELL • Rob WALKER • Michael WEBB • Jeffrey WEISMAN • C. H. WILLIAMS •

Contents

1   Poetry

67   Prose

Poetry

Poetry

5	Life	*Melisa Quigley*
6	Introduction to Philosophy	*Edward O'Dwyer*
8	Never Enough Kudzu	*Elizabeth Buttimer*
9	Father Vladimir's Problems circa 1650	*Lisa Stice*
10	This gentle curve	*Lucy Tyrrell*
12	Lamentation of the Odontochelys	*Karla Linn Merrifield*
13	Whisper	*Michael Estabrook*
14	Atlantic City Blues	*Lisa Rhodes-Ryabchich*
16	Bad Luck	*Jan Chronister*
18	A Blushing Bride	*C. H. Williams*
20	Eggplants	*Shane Guthrie*
21	An American City	*Shawn Aveningo Sanders*
22	The Sunshine of Beer	*Barbara A. Meier*
24	My Friends Call Me Rumpy	*Ken Gosse*
26	Note to the Ex	*Sharron Hough*
28	From Gautama Buddha	*John Lambremont Sr.*
29	Not Too Much to Ask	*Ron Lavalette*
30	Apotheosis	*Howard Brown*
31	My Son Can't Get Enough	*Ruth Sabath Rosenthal*
32	Invisible Finger	*Morgan Driscoll*

34	Mansion full of art	*Chuka Susan Chesney*
36	Baxter Christianson and Perry Percival	*Mark Hudson*
41	Discards	*Gary Beck*
42	Mulberries	*Michael H. Brownstein*
43	Staring at Me	*Tony Daly*
44	Fracking	*Jemshed Khan*
46	Semaphore: Another Self-Elegy	*William Doreski*
48	sky collapse	*Linda M. Crate*
49	Too Much Greed	*Claire Feild*
50	The Rich Die Higher Up	*Ted Mico*
52	W Shakespeare	*DS Maolalai*
54	Pig Generation	*Martin Jon Porter*
57	methodist makeover	*Carl 'Papa' Palmer*
58	Scavengers	*Marsha Mittman*
60	BlurBlurBlur	*Piet Nieuwland*
62	Black in Manhattan	*Dennis Wayne Bressack*
64	I Don't Want To Talk To Anyone Right Now	*Judah Eli Cricelli*

Life

Melisa Quigley

Working long hours
too frightened to complain
buzzing around
like a bee making honey
Social media makes me believe
life is all about stature
and making lots of money
Everyone else appears
to be doing better
I wonder about this
life I am leading
where diamonds sparkle
and gold glitters
bigger cars
and the smell of lovers
I ask myself —
what really matters?
Is it greed or the cost
of living?
One thing's for sure
I feel like I'm sinking

Introduction to Philosopy

Edward O'Dwyer

It's correct to take assignments seriously,
but I once took an Introduction to Philosophy assignment
too seriously. That day, we all left the lecture hall
and went separate ways out into the world
to complete a selfless act.

Our Professor seemed to take great pleasure
in listening to accounts of our good deeds
and then telling us why we all failed.

Picking up soaking hitch-hikers
and pulling up weeds in a stranger's garden
are as self-indulgent as eating a big bowl of ice-cream
when the consequence of not doing so
is an incomplete assignment, a fail,

and so that was the day we learned to distinguish
between selflessness and philanthropy,
to see the gain and guilt
behind what we do and once thought pure.

After many more botched attempts
I eventually traded lives with a homeless man,
selecting him merely because my clothes
would be a good fit on him
after a few weeks of regular, nutritious meals.

I'd spent some time settling into my new life,
his old life, adjusting to its shabbiness
and indignities, and was rattling
some pocket change inside a paper cup

when I recognised a suit approaching.
A suit once mine. It was him, neater, healthier,
expertly groomed, clean-shaven,
and a salon-bestowed sheen on his face.

He didn't seem to know me, didn't acknowledge me
in any way as he went by, and I was determined
to have no feelings about that, none at all,
but couldn't quite stop myself.
Disappointment came in some back door

to my consciousness, raising its bitter voice
about all I'd given, the ingratitude, the amnesia of taking,
and I was agreeing fully, wanting something from him,
anything at all, so long as it wasn't nothing.

Never Enough Kudzu

Elizabeth Buttimer

Fescue, unfettered as pasture,
roams free without fence line
all the way to Mt. Zion Road.
There on the shoulder, kudzu
rambles everywhere, dominates
all that's green. That stubborn vine,
bully of Southern roadsides,
cannot be contained, unsatisfied
with the lion's share of fertile soil,
its greedy tentacles grab
for position, seek nutrition of sun
and soil, as if it's the bully's due.

Unperturbed, Queen Anne's lace
stands its ground. Ivory clusters
reach for the sun, stretch their faces
upward in righteous indignation
at the blasted vine's intrusion,
hard-headed thievery of soil
and space. Usurping of position
continues until free-wheeling
cows escape the neighboring pasture
and discover they can't-get-enough
kudzu, no matter how hard they try.

Father Vladimir's Problems circa 1650

Lisa Stice

It had already been a struggle
to lift his arm
cuffed in heavy fabric
weighted with the power of the Czar,
but to also turn the gold and jewel encrusted
cover of the Bible?
Utter hopelessness,
utter despair.
Oh, God,
Father Vladimir pleaded,
please lift my burden.
And he prayed for the Archangel Michael
to fly off the gilt dividing screen,
with sword and armor to help him,
but thanked God that the screen was there at all
to hide his struggle
from the parishioners,
for how could they
put their faith in someone
who can't even open the Gospel?

This gentle curve

Lucy Tyrrell

west of Red Cliff—
it's my landmark
driving home
on State Highway 13.
Beyond the end
of pink-gray asphalt
(mixed with local sand),
yellow diamond sign
suggests 'Speed 40'
before dark-gray asphalt
snakes past hayfields,
rows of tall red pines.

Telltale laths spear a line
across the inside bend of lanes
through unkempt grasses—
inscriptions with magic marker
foretell destruction,
stapled pink streamers
wind-dance impending
summer highway work.

Greed for speed
will slice through winding—
redacting rural disposition,
character of curve.
I mourn this gentle dark-gray snake
as if it were already clubbed,
hung straight from a ten-penny nail
on fading red barn door.

Lamentation of the Odontochelys

Karla Linn Merrifield

My parade of tortoises slowly passed
dumpsters, landfills, brownfields, slag heaps— aghast

at the garbage'd wastelands of pollution.
We've trudged the eons of evolution

to arrive in silent, solemn protest.
And I, Chelonia, Great Mother, rest

after two hundred fifty years of gains
and losses since the Permian's birth pains.

I'm at the tail end of the cavalcade;
I observe how my Turtle People fade.

My carapace like Earth's thin crust is drowning
& being crushed by the green globe's browning.

My scutes gleaned illegally by sly greed.
I'm meat that does the Hunger Nation feed.

Whisper

Michael Estabrook

You second-guess yourself:
should I take money
out of my life savings
for that trip to Italy
or that fancy-schmancy
entertainment center
with the plush chairs?
When you hear a gentle whisper
"of course you must, my dear,
you owe it to yourself
you only go around once."
And you smile even though
you know it's the Devil talking.

Atlantic City Blues

Lisa Rhodes-Ryabchich

A skinny, tall & greedy man with a nervous tic
Orders a sandwich: "Rare roast beef on a roll"—
Sitting on the red soda fountain stool
Bleary eyed & ravenous,
At Bally's Casino restaurant.

The young waiters have moxie! Such smooth
Operators—they don't even crack
A grimace when the drunks saunter in
Dishing out their exact cooking directions
And then reiterate:
"Don't forget to add the onions!"

An echo of slot machines is heard
Buzzing like a bank safe alarm, leaving
My head spinning, as I sip
Hot coffee, next to a horny man
Who is drooling in sexual delight,
As his girlfriend slowly devours a dish
Of vanilla ice-cream.

I have prepared myself
For this, after observing
A busload of wild bachelors
On the highway, greedily watching
Strip tease videos— celluloid pictures
Pulsating like roaches, in sync
With the flashing neon casino lights,
Awaiting this mob of Tom Cruise Clones.

At a Blackjack table, a co-dependent couple
Scheme— his right hand waves the air
Like a magic wand, before each card is dealt—
Then they roar in laughter together, smiling &
Drinking, after each winning hand, like in a trance.

A despondent man, disgusted by his rotten luck,
Sits alone at the quarter slot machines.
He traveled all the way from New York City
& gambled his entire paycheck & lost.
I ask him for a quarter to try my luck &
He confesses to me: "If I don't give it to you
The casino will get it anyway."

At 4 a.m. on the bus going back home,
Traffic slowed to the red sirens
Of a police car & ambulance.
A small car had overturned &
A heavy-set woman lay on a gurney
Before being covered in white.
Whispers hushed over the bus—
"She was probably a nurse going home
Late & fell asleep at the wheel."

Bad Luck

Jan Chronister

Luck rhymes with a word
I won't use in a poem.
I'm not a prude but
believe a poet should
be able to express a thought
without it. I'll just say
WTF! How did our country
end up like this? Was it

all those saloon mirrors broken
in every Western re-run?
Every black cat that
ran in front of our cars?
Every Friday the thirteenth
since Eden? We forget

Wounded Knee
the Greenwood massacre
Japanese internment camps.
Corporate greed kicks in
when immigrants we
don't want approach
our shores, borders, or
step out of line. It should

come as no surprise
we're cleaning house.
We've had plenty of practice.

A Blushing Bride

C. H. Williams

Her bouquet was bursting,
She wanted them all.
She started with lilies;
The first lot, she pulled.
Then peonies from Polly,
From right under her nose,
Violets from Violet,
And roses from Rose.
Handfuls from gardens,
Scalped patches left bare.
Nine gnomes she knocked over,
Not at all did she care.
Fistfuls of freesias,
Clutched in her hands.
Six sunflowers swiped,
She tortured the land.
Too many to hold now,
A bunch much too big,
Yet her eyes they grew wider,
As she saw one more twig.
She put down her bundle,
And reached for the stick,
Her jaw dropped in shock,
As it reared up and bit.

Not fit for her bunch,
She leapt back with a gasp,
A snake bite packed a punch.
She fell with a yelp,
Landing on her backside,
She called out for help,
But venom had her tongue-tied.
She wept in the corner,
Her bouquet crushed underneath,
She'd flattened her flora,
Nothing left, not one leaf.
The neighbours gathered to see,
The greedy bride to be wed,
On her blanket of flowers,
Already dead.

They ordered a wreath,
Fake flowers and fern,
To sit on her coffin,
To rest by her urn.
And pinned to a bench,
Was a plaque stamped in metal,
Bare ground underneath,
Not one single petal.

Eggplants

Shane Guthrie

I had my hands full of eggplants
But I wanted more eggplants
So I reached a hand with an eggplant
For another
But my fingers were not numerous enough
And my fingers were not long enough
To hold so many at once.

They all fell down and got terribly bruised

An American City

Shawn Aveningo Sanders

In the city of trees,
the canopy blocks the celestial view.
The people here walk in shade,
wear God on their sleeves.

The sacred join in politics,
gossip over a chalice of pinot,
cite lines of the gospel—

quotation notations as safe combinations:
     {three turns left to Chapter}
     {two turns right to Verse}
unlock the tax-exempt vault
         [[[hidden]]]
    in the church basement.

Tourists take photos to post online—
         spires that spiral toward sky,
         another ornate cathedral gate
         locked.

Neglected trees with their bulging roots
form lumpy sidewalk box-springs
beneath faded cardboard beds.

The Sunshine of Beer

Barbara A. Meier

There is sunshine in the taste of beer:
of a June wheat day, blonde grain kissing
the cerealan blue sky, and a 103 temperature
baking the green enamel of a John Deere 55 H combine.

It is the smell of bread brewing on the prairie wind.
The farmer, cabless with his Coors,
babysitting his girls in the bin of the combine,
perched above the churning gears.

There were so many ways to die that day:
in the jaws of the combine, sliding on
cracked vinyl seats without a seatbelt,
riding the tipping truck, dumping wheat
at the grain elevator, hoping the elevator man
would give us a stick of gum.

OSHA never knew and KCSL never cared
about us sipping the last swallow of daddy's beer.
They never knew it was the farmer who died.

Was it the pink mercury treated wheat in the old JD seed drill?
The Barban (carbyne) for the wild oats? Or was it the visit
to Sasebo, Japan, swabbing the deck of radiation?

Death blooms from the seeds
drilled into the ground so long ago.
We are harvested by the deed done wrong,
the accidents unknown, the ignorance of greed.
We become the brewed amber ale drunk down.

My Friends Call Me Rumpy

Ken Gosse

They called him ol' Rumpelstiltskin.
and Mephisto was his next-of-kin,
for he used, on his part,
diabolical art
to make gold from the straw he would spin.

A young lady was given wide fame
by her father who spread the false claim
that from straw she spun gold
(that's the story he sold).
She was merely a pawn in his game.

So the King locked her up in a cell
as a test, and her father said, "Well,
there's a fiend who can help
for the price of a whelp,"
so he rang good ol' Rumpy's doorbell.

Making long-story-short, she agreed,
in her time of most desperate need,
for his skill she would sell
her firstborn to his Hell—
although learning Rump's name kills the deed.

Although demons and villains can't win,
in the best tales they often begin
to get the advantage—
but his rage and rantage
was vain, for the lady did win.

Note to the Ex

Sharron Hough

I have fed your need
Your every greed
But nothing satiates
Your desires and
Burning fires
Nothing can abate
There's no restrain
You manage to drain
All I have to give
You only take
No compromise to make
And that's no way to live
So take it and choke
Don't sit and poke
That shell that's left is mine
If ever you need
To think and grieve
Know that I'll be fine
While you've been consuming
I've been fuming
Plotting my counter strike
You have no money
I'm sorry honey
But I've a balance that I like

So who's weeping now
Not this vengeful cow
I've stripped from you what's dear
I'd return it and more
Except I was your whore
You made that perfectly clear
So I've taken what's due
And between me and you
You're lucky that's all I took
Good luck with your life
Regards your ex-wife
Find yourself a new hooker and cook

From Gautama Buddha
(an acrostic)

John Lambremont, Sr.

Needs supplied to most by Mother Earth;
One receives her gifts and knows their worth.

Torment in the form of love of wealth
Operates to take one's mental health;
Rivers of dollars will not suffice
Restless souls consumed with avarice;
Even when the world's best pearl was found,
Not long before hope had run aground,
Trapped in mud and muck that soon surrounds.

Living life in mad pursuit of cash
Is sure to cause in time one's teeth to gnash;
Killer fascination with bank notes
Exacts turns from fervid to morose.

Go with God and shun the grabber's path;
Recognize you need not make a stash;
Ever will your heart beat in your chest,
Even if you have less than the rest;
Death comes to the "least" and to the "best."

Not Too Much to Ask

Ron Lavalette

All I want is whatever little I
already have. And half of yours.
I mean, you've got plenty,
eh? Way more than you need.
So I'm only asking for half.
Equal shares, y'know?
Fifty-fifty seems right, right?
And his, too, maybe; half of
his and maybe half of hers.
Half of theirs. It's all I need.
It's all I'm asking for. Half.

Apotheosis

Howard Brown

Rapacity, greed, cupidity, it makes no difference which word you choose—they all find apotheosis in the bloated demon called Mammon. And whatever obscene excesses of wealth and power this creature may acquire, even that won't be quite enough.

The world festers with the names of those who worship at the altar of avarice: think Wall Street, predatory lenders, big oil, strip miners, mono culture farmers, agricultural-chemical companies, the plastics industry, clear-cut timber barons, the industrial and financial oligarchs who pillage and pollute the Earth without so much as a by your leave, or kiss my ass…

So, friend, if you should find yourself grasping for just a bit more of anything than you truly need, remember, when there's nothing left to devour, the greedy invariably begin to devour themselves.

My Son Can't Get Enough

Ruth Sabath Rosenthal

of what, according to friends & family, he fills
his studio apartment with. Though hard-pressed
for space, he buys & showcases, buys & stows, greedy
for more & more thrill of finding whatever it is he fancies:

Going from one thrift shop to another, he snatches up
all manner of old silver cutlery, porcelain cats, hatboxes,
a vintage Crock-pot, leaded glass milk bottles, old maps! Why
only yesterday, a chipped Baccarat piggybank nearly broke

his momentum, when the shelf he envisioned it on, was
he knew, questionable. With not an inch of space to spare, I swear,
his out-of-hand obsession for endless acquisition will have him
(& me) packing for the loony bin &, further, filling

his nosey neighbors with even more earfuls of one particular
gossip's mouthfuls: Whenever that biatch sees him schlepping
in parcels, she hits him with "And what have you bought now?
Have you given any thought to how it will fit in an apartment

already filled to the brim with junk? What some poor soul
could do with all the money you waste!" And behind his back
the yenta mieskeit (as he calls her to her face) mimes the word
misfit, while, all the while, overtly patting that very same back of his.

Invisible Finger

Morgan Driscoll

That needle jutting by the bridge,
at least it's not a condom or a tooth.
I found a leather wallet once along the pier,
but that was up around the fucking tourist shops.
Down river here you need some skills to make a score.
The kids will look, or dry rod fishers, or sad folks walking slow.
But dudes like me? There's nothing getting
        by me worth a mother-fucking nickel.
You got a cigarette or something? That sumbitch
        said you'd make this worth my while.
The law been down here yesterday, and now here's
        you with camera crews. I know what's what.
Dude like me don't have too much that I can barter
        with. I need some pay for what I know.
My time's worth something too, least much to
        me. I got other things that I can do.
Hey, just because I look like this don't
        mean I don't got plans or prospects.

Been on camera once already too; night
        Tom's auto shop got torched.
Just say'n, got experience on top of gritty fucking authenticity.
Don't look so shocked, I said I fucking know what's up.
Want some viral hits from this folksy hobo?
It's gonna cost a Grant or more.
This trope's got self-esteem.
Now who's got a match?
Where's my mark?
Shit.

Mansion full of art

Chuka Susan Chesney

owner old
I am invited

Yes I am touring
Warhols and Magrittes
a fiber glass mermaid
floating in pool
I want to take her home

Heiress of the house
provides buffet
I covet her daily organic kale
purified ice in champagne sangria
powerful boats on private lake
the wind whippoorwill of American flag

I sip her money
her taste her Rolls
but never hanker for pulled-taffy cheeks
or the terrapin creases of dilapidated neck

My dwelling is small
no niche for beauty
Her saline fish
skim wall with soothe
My wanna-be existence a congested sinkhole

In art pavilion
are tandem bathrooms
marble walls veined
I can pee in there

Upstairs an octagon
box of Frank Stella
I brush my hand through air
a cavity of greed

Baxter Christianson and Perry Percival

Mark Hudson

There was a rather spoiled child, who grew up in Lake Forest, an affluent suburb of Chicago, named Baxter Christianson. Both his parents were millionaire real estate icons: technically Baxter would never have to work a day in his life. Everything was handed to him on a silver platter.

All the pretty girls liked him, well, not really, they liked him for his money. And he liked them for one reason, sex. He wasn't necessarily like a pimp turning women into prostitutes, he looked at them as objects to be conquered, and he used money to have his desires meet. After a while, it was about as exciting as watching reruns of Gilligan's Island.

Furthermore, his parent's enormous allowance bestowed on him was never quite enough. Using money to fill the bottomless hole in his soul, in high school he created a gigantic drug-dealing business, which made him outrageously wealthy.

Then there was Perry Percival, that annoying pest! Perry was always trying to tag along with Baxter, because he was a high-school nerd, and he wanted to be cool like Baxter. He wanted to be like him, because he was unlucky with the ladies, and he thought some of Baxter's luck could rub off on him. He would take sloppy seconds with these high-school hotties, he was truly a horny young lad!

Baxter just used Perry as a disposable drug dispenser, doing all the dirty work of distributing the drugs, while he gained most of the profits.

So one day, to get rid of Perry, hopefully, he sent Perry all the way to Colorado to pick up a giant order of cocaine. Like a peon, Perry obliged.

But on the way back, Perry got busted with a kilo of cocaine. He was sentenced to seven years of prison, which toughened him up after being a people-pleaser.

He hated prison, and therefore hated Baxter and blamed him for his situation. All he wanted to do was get out and get revenge.

Seven years later Perry was set free, and
Baxter's parents had died, passing unto him the
gigantic mansion in Lake Forest. By now, it
was a non-stop party there, tons of drugs,
and what would be called non-stop orgies.

Perry went to the residence, and he
hadn't forgotten where he lived. Baxter
had completely forgotten about Perry,
he didn't know and didn't care.

So it was quite a shock when Perry
snuck into Baxter's mansion through the
secret passage he knew about-rigged up
with an explosive suicide vest.

He came into the room where
Baxter was selling drugs, and he had
his women "groupies" at his side.
They were half-naked, begging
for more drugs.

Baxter looked at Perry,
half-stoned, "You again?"
Then a moment of clarity came,
and he noticed the suicide vest.
He pressed a button by the
fireplace, and the whole section
of the room spun around like
a carnival ride, or a scene from
a Batman movie or something,
and to Perry's horror, he had
been "whirled" around, and
all that remained was a blank wall.

He must've thought of everything! thought Perry, and before he knew it, prison bars came down from the ceiling, connecting to locks on the floor, imprisoning Perry.

"What's he going to do, call the cops?" thought Perry. "He'll go to jail!"

Baxter must've underestimated the suicidal and homicidal nature of Perry, and his desire to get revenge, even if it meant his own death.

He also underestimated the powerful explosives that were in that vest.

"Oh, what the hell," thought Perry, "I have nothing to lose."

Rather than go back to jail, he pressed the button. Tons of TNT exploded, sending his body and the prison cell bars exploding into the air. That section of the mansion was a blaze of fire, and Perry was dead in a second.

But Baxter, who was watching on his many cameras in his safe room, where he looked for cops, was not expecting this.

His "groupies" screamed for help, but Baxter raced out, leaving them to die. He took a bullet-proof elevator down to his "get-away car," which was just there in case he had to get away, and put the keys in the ignition.

But once again, he underestimated Perry's desire for revenge. The minute he put the keys in the ignition, explosives blew the car to smithereens.

Perry pretty much had a general idea how things would go. For once he covered his bases. The mansion burned for a long time before anyone even noticed, because rich people in Lake Forest don't have much contact with their neighbors. The fire department came, and by then, the mansion was a pile of rubble.

They rebuilt a house on the property, and some say it's haunted by people from the past, their ghosts.

Well, you know what the saying is. There goes the neighborhood.

Discards

Gary Beck

In a corrupt city
of increasing poverty
children of the homeless
are a low priority
for diminishing resources,
struggled over by factions
focused on their own needs,
unconcerned that throwaway kids
are discarded by the thousands,
victims of democracy.

Mulberries

Michael Brownstein

No, chipmunk of the field; no, vole; no, raccoon;
no, possum; no, overweight groundhog; no,
squirrel of the eaves; no, house wrens of the bricks;
no, walking stick; no, red ant; no, spongy field
of weeds and litany, mold and swamp beetle; no—
All of these are mine. Lakshmi gave them to me
and you cannot have any. If I want to harvest one
hundred, two hundred, three hundred a day,
an hour, a minute, so be it. If I want five hundred
and wish to leave four hundred baking into spoilage,
too bad. Lakshmi gave them to me—me—
and I am not going to share. Don't climb my tree,
don't flit into its interior light, don't dishonor its leaves,
its limbs, don't discolor its bark, its twigs, its soul—
I own all of the mulberries and I do not want to share.

Staring at Me

Tony Daly

Eyes begin to shine
Throat begins to whine
A raised foreleg
You begin to beg
Lips begin to stretch
Poor little wretch
Nose upon my thigh
Greedy gleam to eye
Your hunger is an act
Your stomach is not wracked
My hand is set
A friendly pet
Hunger subsides
When friendship's implied

Fracking

Jemshed Khan

*"Lithosphere." Def. Rigid, rocky outer layer of the Earth
consisting of the crust.*
– https://www.britannica.com

    be with me
    when senses wake
    to the bed's

    shaking frame,
    the ground rumbling
    underfoot

    as a fault line
    slips and widens up
    to swallow us,

    as needles twitch
    on the Richter scale
    at the shifting

    between
    tectonic plates.
    we could shout,

*No fracking
in the lithosphere!*
or just lie

in bed and say,
*While it lasted, the sex
was great.*

either way,
we're burning down
our last cigarette.

Semaphore: Another Self-Elegy

William Doreski

At Park Street the greasy scent
of popcorn stokes the hunger
of lunch-hour crowds. The glare

ripples with exhaust. Winter
has toppled into spring without
withdrawing its quotient of snow.

I walk as slowly as possible.
In a sixth-floor room my dentist
conspires with his instruments

to unman my fondest moments
and leave me mentally beached
on a bleak shore north of Iceland.

Not pain, but the blank oppression
of being warped into a pose
for an hour or two in his chair.

How often I've stumbled into grief
with my wallet in my pocket
fluttering like a trapped canary.

How often I've paid to dignify
whatever's best kept hidden
while fog muffles the groaners

in Boston Harbor, and buses
idle in diesel stinks outside
airport terminals shuddering

with massive sums of luggage.
I should abandon the shadows
I cast on filthy city sidewalks

since people mistake them for me.
The dentist plans to extract
something essential and leave me

hollow as an unknown language.
His touch lacks empathy, but snuffed
with Novocain I won't notice

that his clumsiest gestures suggest
the semaphore code I learned
in Sea Scouts. And I won't know

until later to which entity,
warped by a greed for worship,
these awkward signals refer.

sky collapse

Linda M. Crate

i mistook lust for love,
and death for life and unkindness for kindness;
thought the sirens in your eyes were mermaids
a song of kindness and compassion
that would save me from troubled waters—
however, you were simply
greed
as you wanted every part of me for free;
couldn't afford me
but you were hungry for every piece of me that
wouldn't cost you a thing
because you were selfish with your love
which was really lust you would admit later because
nothing you gave me was sincere—
your greed needed, wanted me
until there was someone more convenient to lay upon
your bed and kiss your eyes to sleep;
but one day your nightmares will consume you until there's
nothing left
try to imagine how that feels
i know it may be hard because you have no imagination
a collapsing sky
has more empathy than you ever did.

Too Much Greed

Claire Feild

The woman prances down the street with
   her right hand dangling, four diamond
   rings on four fingers, respectively.

And the children beg for food in Mexico.

The man in Alaska carries bags of dead animals
   over the ice to his log cabin home. He will
   have plenty to eat for the winter, enough
   to keep his belly pregnant.

And the children look for water in Africa.

Her hands are itchy, for her billions of dollars
   do not satisfy her munificent personality.

*And the children in Syria run from bombs and
   nerve gas.*

The greenhouse protects the plants as best it
   can, and no pesticides are used.

*The owner of the greenhouse and plants buys
   too many plants as he is thinking of
   the next plant he will purchase as he
   plants the plant he cuddles in his hands,
   preparing it for its too small home.*

The Rich Die Higher Up

Ted Mico

This is a math test
           but do not use your pencils.
If she weighs less than an eighth
           of a donkey, how many donkeys
           does it take to buy baby Jenny?
She's just learnt to wash herself
           but does not bear weight
           how much extra?
How many teenage Jennys
           for that fresh skyscraper
           tickling the air
           with one penthouse plus security.
Subtract that number from the office block next door
           stood up with greed,
           unwashed below whooping revolt
           around recycling bins.
Is Jenny prettier recycled
           or in fresh pajamas?
           Do we get more stories
           if she turns our way?

How many false positives
        will bring teen Jenny
        and those derelict lips
        back from *ohs*?
Less than a handful of vertigo pills
        to make that penthouse
        less frightening?
Which is the greater of Aristotle's uses for Jenny:
        her intended purpose
        or her bartered value?
If older Jenny sells herself
        to the highest story, what lengths
        will we go to in order to buy her childhood back?
Congratulations, would a slap on the back
        one hard thwack be enough
        to make both Jenny's eyes fall out?
How many backs will it take
        to blind us into seeing Jenny
        as a sign from God reading
        Closed for renovation.
How many slaps
        to convince her shoulder blades
        they should sprout wings instead.

W Shakespeare

DS Maolalai

eh
he wrote them for money
like tv writers today.
very much in the mold
of tv writers
actually,
all cheap stuff,
all to turn a profit.
and yes,
he slipped some poetry
in there too
but you can tell
he liked his sonnets better,
otherwise
why would he have
wrote
in such constricting form?
he could have done a play
and got it all else out
much more grandly
but there was no money
in that.

he had a family
I guess —
his wife
got his bed —
and once
he was a witness
in some trial.
I don't know
anything else about him.
strange,
we all put such import on someone
who still had organs
and took shits,
except
I quite liked
Hamlet
I suppose,
but why
would that matter
peanuts
to anyone
in the cheap seats?
he wrote plays.
it was easy.
if he'd wanted people
to like him
he could have been a carpenter
instead
and made
v. comfortable
chairs.

Pig Generation

Martin Jon Porter

"Of what use or sense is an immortality of piggishness?"
Captain Wolf Larsen – *The Sea-Wolf*, by Jack London

I

pigs
scampering into their private pens
closing the gate
without oinking to neighbours

pigs
putting mud into trotters of other pigs
yet squealing behind their tails

pigs
with 310 degrees of vision
still slaughtering shoulders
of other animals
as they walk past

II

pigs
in trough restaurants
eating 3% of their body weight

pigs
in trough cafés and bars
drinking 10% of their body weight

pigs
that keep fattening after Christmas
from no exercise

III

pigs
trampling on vegetation
not using their manure
to fertilise re-growth

pigs
clogging up roads
in expensive trucks
instead of using public transport

IV

pigs
with noses skyward
sniffing the next market

pigs
snorting
the value of their crackle

pigs
working day and night
at the expense of their piglets
so they can afford two-storey pens

V

pigs
window shopping
on public holidays

are pigs
that fly

methodist makeover

Carl 'Papa' Palmer

the huge pile of clothes donated to our church
rummage sale by the war widow her departed
husband a young man just forty four his taste
ran fairly medium along with his size 34 X 32
trousers brown blue tan gray and black Dockers
16 ½ X 34 button down shirts and knit pullovers
to keep the wives away from the pile of clothes
my size the rumor emerges these clothes were
salvaged from state funeral homes taken off
dead men after their viewing everyone knows
the body is always buried naked all my size I
won't try on a single piece of my new wardrobe

Scavengers

Marsha Mittman

the mountains loom large
not pine laden and fragrant

nor craggy and awe inspiring
rather huge piles of garbage

that daily grow higher
foul rotting reeking

of human waste and remnants
and the women children

greedily dig through the
odiferous malignant heaps

for any prize piece of cloth
object wood metal to sell or

worse for a rotting morsel
to eat starved as they are

with blisters and open sores
on their hands and feet

where constant contact is made
and the seagulls natural

scavengers of the trash
fly about competing for food

the gulls ultimately having
the choice and ability to leave

but without skills money education
human scavengers, the untouchables,

are relegated to – and as – garbage
                                              for life

BlurBlurBlur

Piet Nieuwland

We are in, as the tee shirt full frontal states, Tokyo, London, New York, Dargaville

The Great Northern Wairoa bulges like a big fat eel, the incoming tidal wave swallows the overflowing breakfast menu of eggs free range, focaccia wholemeal, beans and sweet hot kumara

A triple shot expresso saxophonist trills, tribbles, vibrates a spill out a resonant jazz jive that opens all walls

The chalk board invites patrons to a little greedy indulgence, servings of rich chocolate orange berry cake with cream that mirrors a vivid red cow abstractly in celebration of kiwi roaming free though pastoral landscapes

Sunday morning main street vibe is a liquor store open and a gaggle of swaggering locals out back, the garden courtyard filled with banana palms and boasts

Buoyant putangitangi chicks hang ten on a Hokusai wave over Riporipo beach

Rafts of ghost kauri logs snake the afternoon rollin' down the river, dodging the jingle bell rock and carols bleeding from the scorched wasted hills

The clouds are intercontinental, in a slow motion parade to and from the horizon just over there to Bondi, or Manly and the beach babes here as sweet as any there, any on the Vie De Pacifique Perimeter anywhere

Black in Manhattan

Dennis Wayne Bressack

Black is the color. The mannequins wear
very little summer orange yellow green.
Even though the pavement is percolating,
fashion is always more important than comfort.

An old black man in a tattered winter coat
ragged gloves and plastic bag boots
begs on an empty garbage can
in front of a Starbucks window

where blind upward mobile executives
with cell phones and ipod ear plugs
sip grande latte café and
mocha cappuccino espressos.

Young black men from above ninety-sixth
service the upper west side crust
in the Sunday morning dress down
New York Times Parade.

Invisible walls separate patrons
attired in expensive designer jeans
and hair colors that God couldn't create.
They stare out the window at

black women who push white babies in
brand name strollers past
wheelchairs with grandmas who sell
old books for 50 cents each.

At 10 P.M business meetings
the sidewalks vibrate with chirping cells
as wheeler dealers devour grotesque meals
for $100 apiece.

The waiter's uncle, paper cup in hand,
begs for his small piece of the pie.
The dishwasher's sister, asleep in the park,
prays that her baby won't die.

I Don't Want To Talk To Anyone Right Now

Judah Eli Cricelli

Customer record.
Press, press
Lumine
Stress
L.E.D. lows,
The quiet corners,
Things you chose,
You're in my room,
The godhead sheds
Its womb—
The corners
Room for others,
No more room, fluoresce
And fade and lose
Some weight,
The choice you made
Seems overplayed—
My stomach turns
And fingers burn
From all the typing.
Screws,
The things you lose

You choose
But you're still bruised
And mostly
All shut up inside
But they won't
See the scratches
On your thighs
Or be there on the highs
Or close
The door,
Become a
Connoisseur
Of those
Burnt-up feelings,
I'm fake
You're real
The same old deal
'Cause I can't feel
Right now—
Speak,
Breathe.
Hold,
Then heave
And
Talk—
To me—

In 1s—
And 0s—
The coffee was bad, and
I was mad,
You laugh, it's sad
But then
My words are fragile,
Flat
And faint,
I type
But my replies
Come late
And voices now, they're
In the dark
There's voices in
The dark,
They see the
Things that be,
The hole in me
And all the greed—
It's what you are and
What you need—
But when you find the room to breathe
The voices will recede.

Prose

Prose

71	Toast	*Nod Ghosh*
75	Modern Politics of Equality	*M Pauseman*
77	Plunder	*Caroline Smadja*
81	Making Up Time	*Niles Reddick*
83	Moving Up	*Foster Trecost*
85	The Proposal	*Salvatore DiFalco*
86	Poor Frank	*David Rae*
89	Southern Breakfast	*Mike Lewis-Beck*
91	Something Snapped	*Wayne Scheer*
94	Brotherly Love	*Paul Beckman*
98	Fake Eunuch	*Robert Scotellaro*
100	Goodness and Mercy	*Linda Tyler*
105	Place Your Bets	*Jim Bell*
108	Small Sweet Thing	*Alex Reece Abbott*
110	The Sugar Assassin	*Jo Davies*
112	The Booth	*Andrew Grenfell*
116	Lieberman	*Larry Lefkowitz*
120	An Exceptional Young Whine	*Peter Lingard*
123	Nothing in This Truck is Worth Dying For *Jonathan Slusher*	
126	Boom or Bust	*Irene Buckler*
127	Enemies	*Joe Mills*

131	Haunting Our Hearts and Pocketbook	*Meryl Baer*
135	Catch a Tiger	*Cynthia Leslie-Bole*
139	Going Commerical	*Andrei Konchalovsky*
	translation	*Bryon McWilliams*
141	Sons and Silkworms	*Christine Johnson*
145	The Recent History of the Sánchez Family Tragedies: Part III	*Guilie Castillo Oriard*
149	Jeb, Earl and the Gopher	*Steven Carr*
153	Gunfight at the Shopping-Cart Corral	*Alan C. Baird*
156	The Return of Red Ledbetter Episode 3	*JP Lundstrom*
161	Set for Life	*Copper Rose*
165	Sunday	*Edward Reilly*
169	The Promise	*Abha Iyengar*
171	Gaslighter in the Morgue – Touching Up Beauty	*Alison Fish*
175	Greed – Good or Bad?	*Jeffrey Weisman*
177	Through a glass, darkly	*Rob Walker*
180	Chaos Theory	*Michael Webb*

Toast

Nod Ghosh

"Make us a cup of tea, could you?"

"Okay," I said. I'd come to expect your demands.

You put my guitar down and stretched like an eel on the sofa. Your sweatshirt, several sizes too large, hid the curves of your body. But I knew what lay underneath. To a certain extent, that's what kept me going. I was your puppy-slave, rewarded with sexual favours.

Back then I'd have done anything for you despite your complacency. In the kitchenette, I filled the kettle, and wished I could crush the ennui that had grown between us. Your nonchalance should have been a turn off. Instead, it made me want to bite you all over.

I didn't have time for your demands.

Could you fix the derailleur on my bike?
I could really do with some shelves putting up in my room.
I have at interview at eight tomorrow morning. You could take me.

I needed to write my thesis, but you wanted me in large doses. When you had what you needed, you took more.

"Do you have any bread?" you called out. "I could kill for a piece of toast."

"Toast?"

"Yeah," you said. "Toast with no crusts. And have you got anything to go on it?"

"I have marmite." I walked back into the lounge while the water boiled.

"Got any cheese?" You gave me an appealing smile. "I could murder some cheese on toast."

"No cheese." I wanted to lie next to you and smell you, lick you, sink my teeth into your flesh. I wanted to push my fingers through the russet of your hair and force a scream from you — but I resisted.

"Aw. Don't suppose you could go out and get some cheddar could you?"

"It's late," I said. "The shop will have closed."

"Bugger," you said, like it was my fault. You opened a journal to look for jobs, stabbing a pen on the pages, circling and ticking. You'd been looking for a year, but hadn't found anything.

"Toast coming up," I said. "Do you want marmite?"

"No. Just toast," you said as I walked out of the room.

I brought tea and toast on a tray.

"Shame about the cheese." You pulled your sweatshirt up, exposing skin. "Could you rub my back? Usual place. It's killing me."

"I'll do it in a second," I said. I needed to re-draft my conclusion. The shared telephone in the corridor rang, and I hoped someone from one of the other flats would answer it.

They didn't.

I shuffled my papers with one hand, massaged your back with the other.

The ringing stopped after several minutes. Then started again.

*   *   *

It had taken years for you to take me for granted. Our passion reignited every time our on and off relationship started again.

I was close to finishing my post-grad. Employers had already shown an interest, and I knew my future was looking good. Jobs in my field, like most, were scarce in those days. It was worse for you. Your career was set on the back burner, and I knew you were losing interest in your field. I was afraid you'd also lose interest in me.

It's not like what we have is anything serious, you'd say.

But it was to me.

You took what you wanted from me. You were greedy for whatever was on offer. But you rarely gave anything back.

The allure of surprise had gone. I'd allowed you to settle into an uneasy comfort, confident I'd always be there for you.

Then I broke our unwritten rule.

I showed you my true feelings. I said I would always love you. I wanted us to be together. I asked you to come away with me. A new beginning. I would look after you.

I gave you the upper hand.

You said you weren't sure, said you needed your freedom.

But later, you still allowed me to crawl on top of you like nothing had happened. I licked you out and made you come. I lay back, expecting you to return the favour. You swept toast crumbs off the sofa and complained.

You left me desperate and hungry.

I watched you roll away, folding and straightening like an earthworm. You wriggled and dropped to the uncarpeted floor with a thud and headed towards the bathroom.

"See you in a minute," you murmured, my black slippers on your feet. And though I hated your selfishness, the ordinariness of your actions, I began to miss you. You'd vacated a space where there had been warmth. It was rapidly cooling to my touch. I ached for you, and it was delicious. I knew the only way I could make our love endure, would be by increasing the distance between us. To discard you, so you'd come crashing back, desperate, thirsty. Hurting because you needed me so much.

I lit a cigarette, pulled my jacket and jeans on. I slipped out of the house as the toilet flushed.

The black-haired woman was at the bar with a bunch of other student-types. She walked backwards right into me. Her strange dark-light skin turned brick red in the glow of the Royal Park lights. I think she was blushing. The thought turned me on. She said something about having seen me coming out of your block of flats a couple of times – said she thought I might know you. *Only vaguely,* I told her. She had no idea what you were to me, or I to you.

I drank a couple of pints and seduced her.

I seduced your friend.

And later I married her.

You see, I too, was greedy for more than I had.

I hope you understand that now, even though you want more than I can give.

"I have responsibilities," I say, climbing out of your bed. Toast crumbs stick to my skin. I make sure I brush them off before I go home.

Modern Politics of Equality

M Pauseman

I want a house on the hills, and

I want you to build it.

I want you to paint it yellow, to remind me of my riches. The ones you will never see.

I want you to do it cheaply, so you can go back to your small shack feeling rewarded. You helped me, and that is what you want.

I want to be able to sit on my balcony, look over my grounds and laugh. For while I look at my car collection in the driveway, you ride on a bicycle to mow my lawns.

I want to prove Marx wrong.

I want to know, hear and see everything that is going on, so you will install cameras for my pleasure. You don't want privacy.

I want to charge you rent, for living in my view.

I want to knock down the city and build it new, as a park, so I can stroll through at my own leisure. But fear not, you will install benches.

I want a wall, so I can lean over it.

I want a swimming pool, so I can fill it with custard and swim in it.

I want what is yours, you have no need for possessions. I will have a room devoted to statues with what were your pensions, and fill it with works from unknown artists.

I want to lay with your daughters on Persian rugs.

I want more than the world can provide, and you will go in search of it for me. Because, what I want is more important than what you need.

Plunder

Caroline Smadja

After my first year back in Paris, I put my lovely home in the Inner Sunset up for sale. I had less than three weeks in San Francisco to pack my belongings of twenty years. In spite of my spartan tastes, the living room boasted a couch, a rattan chair with wrought iron armrests, a potted yucca as large as a palm tree, my ex-husband's piano, and a dhurrie we'd bought at an auction in Marin. Living like a nomad implies no material attachment. Yet that rug, which looked exactly like the one in my mind's eye, pastel flower motifs over a cream background, meant a lot to me. For its sake, I'd switched over to a leave-your-shoes-at-the-door policy that holds to this day.

An estate sale would have yielded hundreds of dollars. Instead, I decided to give most everything away. I asked my close friend Winston to pick first. He chose a huge clay vase that belonged to my ex – who'd declined to take anything – and at my urging, a few serving plates as well. Winston asked me to set them aside for him. I used stickers to write his name on each. Kirk, my oldest friend in California and a former cook, took the *Cuisinart* and other kitchen utensils. Weeks later, he was still thanking me profusely. Other friends came by. Some left with a thing or two. Others only wished me luck with all the packing that lay ahead.

On the afternoon Ashley visited, no one had claimed the living room furniture and paraphernalia. The piano was the only piece I was hoping to sell. Though I'd long felt Ashley and I hadn't grown any closer after two decades than after a couple of months, a disturbing discovery for my European self, I extended the same offer to her as to other friends.

She zeroed in on the huge clay vase set in a corner. "This one's reserved," I said. Next, she saw a deep blue ceramic bowl on the kitchen counter. I told her Winston was also taking that. She pouted. "All the best stuff's been claimed already." Her comment gave me pause. Yet, I did my utmost to make up for her disappointment. We agreed she would take the dining table and matching chairs, the yucca and the big pot of lavender I'd bought in my feeble attempt at home-staging.

She next asked for the dhurrie rug. I was planning to have it shipped to Paris later. I offered to loan it to her in the meantime. "It wouldn't feel right to part with it once I'd have put it in my home," she replied. Again, this gave me pause. "Let's forget about the dhurrie," I only said. "It's the one thing I want to keep."

On the day I flew back to Paris where a new teaching job awaited me, the house stood fully furnished. I'd managed to empty every shelf of books and objects, to box or discard all the stuff my ex and I had stored in the basement, and had given my beloved Honda Accord to charity. I'd asked my neighbor and dear friend Margie to give the keys to the real estate agent and to keep an eye out on my behalf. A seventy-five-year-old woman as feisty as she was diminutive, Margie had adopted me a decade earlier the moment I'd knocked at her door to introduce myself. Throughout my divorce, she often played surrogate mom to me.

The sale went astonishingly fast. I got twice the price we'd bought the house for in the early '90s. If I still had it today, I'd be sitting on a million dollars. I did my best to keep track of the process by phone and email. A few weeks after my return to Paris, Margie called me in a panic.

"Honey, I think your home has been burglarized. I walked in this morning. All the furniture's gone."

I called my agent ASAP. The day before, she'd handed the keys over to her young assistant, she admitted when pressed. "My assistant told me a friend of yours came by to pick up some items. She assumed you two had an understanding."

I had to piece the rest of it together long distance. Ashley had driven up in a U-Haul truck and taken what we'd agreed upon plus the piano, the wrought iron chair, Winston's clay vase with his name on it, the stereo system I'd promised my painter.

And the dhurrie rug.

"I have no word for that," I told Margie when we spoke again.

"I do. That's called plunder!"

After days of wrestling with my initial shock, I resolved to ask for the clay vase and the rug back – I didn't bother with the stereo or the piano that weighed tons – and lost further sleep over it. How do you treat a grown woman with no lack of money who, not content to take the freebies you gave with pleasure, grabs everything in sight, including presents to other people?

It took me over two hours to pen my request. My letter started with: "I'm so sorry about the misunderstanding." I could find no 'I'm sorry' in Ashley's reply. She'd consulted with the young real estate assistant before hauling things away, she wrote. She returned the clay vase and the dhurrie, as requested, but volunteered none of the other stuff. A week later, a friend of hers who was to host me in Berlin sent a brief note informing me he wouldn't be in town after all.

This hardly came as a surprise. I did wonder what story she'd told him to make herself the wronged party. Then again, as the French are prone to saying: *Les absents ont toujours tort.* Those who are away always turn out wrong.

Making Up Time

Niles Reddick

Truth be known, Brad and Sandy had spent well over a hundred thousand dollars trying to have a baby, and nothing had worked, so they went all the way to China, got them a beautiful little girl, but the husband didn't want her to grow up alone; the wife didn't care about that and didn't want a second child.

Through a variety of circumstances, they ended up with a boy who'd been put up for adoption because his daddy was in jail for crack and his mama was dead from drugs. Grandparents couldn't take on any more because of bad knees and backs, being emotionally spent from their children on drugs, and making up time they'd spent working their entire lives. "We'd do it if we could," one grandparent told Brad and Sandy, and the couple paid and signed all the forms for the agency, knowing there were probably a few issues.

A few issues turned into more than a few and then into a lot in just the first six months, and Sandy's greed filtered up in her emotions, she felt cheated, and she wanted to give the child back, but Brad wouldn't hear of it. He believed he could make a difference and mold the boy into something good. Sandy thought they should send him off to a mental hospital in advance of his growing up and doing drugs.

Unfortunately just five years into adoption, Brad had a massive heart attack, leaving Sandy with a son she'd never wanted and didn't want to deal with and a daughter who was no trouble at all. She tried here and there, so she could tell folks she tried. By the time the boy was thirteen, he experimented with drugs and when he was fourteen, he killed himself, but not before he shot his adopted mother when she told him she wanted him out of her life, so she could make up time she'd lost on him. Both were cremated and Lindsey moved in with her adopted grandparents until she graduated high school, took her inheritance, and moved to Atlanta to begin a new life and attend college.

Moving Up

Foster Trecost

Sometimes I had the time right and sometimes the place, but never both. A while back they finally showed up together, and I got promoted.

From the outside, The Express looked pretty plain. Gray metal doors, two of them. But behind those doors, that's where it got interesting. The carriage was bigger than the others, and trimmed in mirrors and brass. A chandelier hung up top and tiny marble squares tiled the floor. Maybe the most extravagant elevator ever built, she pulled passengers to the sky lobby, forty-eight floors up.

These assignments aren't doled out to just anyone. Seasoned operators, that's who gets them. Elderly men with an easy demeanor achieved only through aging. And Carlson had aged plenty. He was the perfect elevator man, knew his riders by name, knew who had children, who had grandchildren. He had both.

I'd been stuck in Bank B for fourteen months, which was long enough to know I needed more than *"What floor, Sir,"* and *"Where today, Ma'am."* I didn't know their names, didn't want to know, but I knew I needed more. After a few trips, I decided I'd had enough. I made my way to the man in charge, but not because someone filed a complaint. This time I was going to get a raise, or I was going to quit.

This was about the time Carlson closed his doors. He'd just greeted everyone and asked about their weekends. "Next stop, sky lobby," he said, and the elevator started to rise, but about half way up, he decided he'd had enough, too.

In his wordless way, the man in charge asked what I wanted, but before I could say his phone rang. He picked it up, listened, and hung up, and there was no way me or anyone else could've known he'd just been informed of Carlson's untimely passing. "Report to The Express," he said. "You've been promoted. I don't know why you're here, but the job's yours. I suggest you take it."

Right time, and right place, and I've been running The Express ever since. I'm sorry Carlson had to die, he was a decent man in every way: *"Next stop, sky lobby,"* were his last words, and I'm sure they rang about as true as anything he'd ever said.

The Proposal

Salvatore DiFalco

Nino the goat had brought the village great prosperity with his ability to predict outcomes of Serie A soccer games—achieved by way of pasteboard and hoof placement. The villagers had pooled their resources and made a killing with city bookies. A new fountain had been installed in the piazza, and a statue of St. Rocco, the village's patron saint, was being chiseled at that moment by a renowned regional sculptor, Martino Bracchi, who promised a masterwork—but Father Carmine, the village priest, was dubious. All this ill-gotten money had made the village more bearable, true, but there's always a downside. Furthermore, and this is where perhaps he failed as a villager but succeeded as a man of the cloth, he didn't trust Nino. Goats were connected to Satan, it was inescapable. Moreover, who names a goat? It was unnatural. One morning, Father Carmine approached a destitute man known as Lupo by the villagers. Dark, hirsute, with menacing red eyes, Lupo would do anything for a few lira. After Father Carmine made his proposal, Lupo looked at him sideways. "You want me to off the goat?" he said. "Yes," Father Carmine said, "he's evil." Lupo burst out laughing. "Evil?" he said, "but he predicted that Palermo would beat Juventus! You call that evil? Please." When Lupo, also known as the village gossip, told everyone about the proposal, no less than seven attempts were made on the priest's life. Nino correctly predicted that the eighth attempt would be the last.

Poor Frank

David Rae

When Mum came back from the market, the boot of the car was filled with big boxes of shopping that had to be carried into the house. Dad said that me and Frank should help him. So we helped carry the shopping while Dad went and watched rugby on the television.

Eventually, it seemed as if we had finally moved all the shopping. I said to Frank that we should close the boot lid and go and play, but he said that there was still food in the boot. I looked but could not see anything, and he said that there was a bar of chocolate right at the back of the car boot and that I needed to get into the boot to reach it. I always liked to be helpful, so I was only too happy to help. I climbed into the boot and reached as far back as I could and then Frank closed the boot lid tight, and I was trapped in the dark. Frank had played a trick on me.

Frank was always playing tricks. I wasn't frightened in the car boot. I thought that the joke was on Frank because I could eat the chocolate bar all to myself instead of sharing it with him. But there wasn't a chocolate bar at all. It was very dark in the car boot, and even though I shouted and banged on the lid, Frank never opened it. Eventually, he got bored, and after I promised not to be mad, he opened the boot.

I told Frank he was being mean to play a trick like that. But he said it was just a joke and that no harm was done. I said that it was very dark in the car boot. He asked me if I was afraid of the dark and I said no. Well, there you are then he said, why are you making such a big fuss? I said that there could be spiders in the boot and he said there wasn't and anyway if it was such a big deal he would get into the boot and show me that there was nothing to be afraid of.

Frank climbed into the boot, and I closed the lid. I asked him if he wanted to come out and he said no that it was fine in there. He bet me he could stay in the boot much longer than I did and not be a cry baby about it. I asked if he wouldn't rather come out and go and play, and he said no thanks he was quite happy where he was.

Just then Granny came down the path. It was time for lunch, and she had made soup that had to be eaten now before it got cold and none of my nonsense, just come right now she said. But Granny, I said Frank is in the boot of the car, and I can't just go away and leave him. What nonsense she told me; Mum should do something about that overactive imagination of mine and that I shouldn't go telling lies to my own dear Granny who was not long for this life. I tried to tell her again and moved towards the car and shouted, but Frank just kept silent, so she grabbed me and pulled me into the kitchen and put a plate of hot soup in front of me and told me to eat it all or else.

There were four soup plates on the kitchen table, and the girls were eating two of them, and that left one for Frank. Granny asked where Frank was and once again I told her that he was in the boot of the car. Granny glared at me and told me not to tell lies. But I wasn't lying because Frank really was in the boot of the car.

Granny and my two sisters who had finished eating their soup went out and looked for Frank. They shouted on him up the hill and in the tool shed. They looked under the laurel hedge and in the garage. But of course, they never found Frank in any of those places because he was in the car boot like I said he was.

When they let me leave the table to look for Frank, I raced straight to the car. Poor Frank had been in the boot for a very long time. He had been crying and had been wiping his eyes with his hands, and they were all dirty. Granny was very cross and said that I was very wicked to have locked Frank in the car boot and that he could have died in there because there was no air, or that it could have gotten very hot and that I was just lucky that it had been raining all morning. She took Frank to the kitchen, and after he ate his soup which Granny heated up for him, she took an apple and peeled and cut it up into little slices and fed them to him dipped in brown sugar while he sat on her knee. Eventually, she said I could eat the apple peel, but that she hoped it choked me.

I told Frank I was sorry, but he only looked at me angrily, even after I told him that it was better to forgive than to receive. When Mum and Dad found out, they were very angry too and blamed me. For at least three days, everyone was angry with me, and when Dad divided up the bar of chocolate that he had bought at the supermarket, the real one not the one that Frank had pretended was in the back of the car, I never got any and he gave mine to Frank which was okay because Frank would have tricked me out of it anyway, and it made me feel a little bit better about what I did to poor Frank.

Southern Breakfast

Mike Lewis-Beck

Elbowing the copper-top counter at the Ruby Slipper thinking on the breakfast poem I was going to write in this greasy spoon in New Orleans, I ponder ordering my test meal of two fried eggs basted, a cooking technique I discovered— upon ordering *The Southern Breakfast*— they did not know about: flip the grease over the yolk to leave a grey-pink patina, leaving the egg glistening like a jelly fish in the sun. Maybe it's not a *southern* thing. The waitress asked if it would be OK to do them some sort of over easy way— "would you get mad, hon?"— and I said "no" and thought also that this was the Big Easy so maybe I should have said over easy in the first place, thinking this over as I read her turquoise T-shirt explaining 'You can't drink all day if you don't start in the morning,' the morning greed thing growing as I stared at the Bloody Marys they were making with a strip of bacon for a swizzle stick, the swizzle stick scoring the philosophical T-shirt imperative, an imperative deflected by the arrival of my coffee mug advertising Poydras Trucking, the coffee itself flagged like a golf course hole, but with a teaspoon. Still the coffee was really tasty, coating my palate for *The Southern Breakfast*: two fried eggs (done somehow), apple-wood bacon, grits, brown butter, a fried green tomato, and a buttermilk biscuit.

This sounded *southern* to me and I was ready to tuck in when it came but the eggs put me off because they had a crinkling brown necklace around them and were snotty(!) on top. I ate them anyway, soaking up the viscosity with the too-big biscuit, starting to feel bad about the *southern* thing when a clean blonde lady sat next to me at the copper-top counter and asked if the cook would toast a bagel from her purse. This was cheeky but she looked cheeky— what my Aunt Mavis would call a 'rich bitch'— she in her tight sphinx hairdo, her pressed cream cotton blouse cleaved just right, tailored pearl slacks, and scarlet flats, a gold-button navy blazer resting over her shoulders. Pampered money with an eating disorder. Why Wasn't She Chowing Down?

Suddenly, I felt better about my meal because I was eating it all, including the grits— just right— and bacon was best ever, I'd never even had a fried green tomato. Then the cook came out, said: "I toast dis bagel," but that she should know other things got toasted in the toaster too so she might not want to, like— *Warning may contain peanuts*— "you know, baby?" She said: "toast my bagel." Everyone happy. That's *southern* hospitality if I'd ever seen it. I woulda thrown her out.

Something Snapped

Wayne Scheer

I was a product of the if-it-feels-good-do-it sixties, but when my son came home from middle school saying that his friend, Wynona, caught her mother in bed with her father's girlfriend, I said, "Enough!" I ripped through the house, tearing Dead posters and flushing a perfectly good half-ounce. I even brought my caftan to Goodwill.

It was almost the 1980s, and I was determined to enter the new decade as an adult.

I knew the transition was going to be difficult. Rachel, my love partner, whose dark hair sashayed past her waist while her bra-less breasts bounced freely under her tie-dye T-shirt, worried.

She feared I was becoming a Republican.

I even cut my hair, greased and combed it straight back. Instead of admiring the chutzpah of Abbie Hoffman and Jerry Rubin, I began quoting William F. Buckley, Jr.

"I don't know you," she'd say. "It's like someone kidnapped my old man and replaced him with a Young American for Freedom. You look like you've gone through Reagan deprogramming and come out a stock broker named Brad."

The change was particularly difficult for our son, Jade. One day I picked him up from school in my VW bug with my "Teach Your Children Well" bumper sticker, and the next day I owned a Volvo station wagon. The hardest part was convincing him to call me Dad. Until then, he called me by my first name to avoid power labels and encourage a democratic upbringing.

We had bought a small home in Santa Clarita, just north of Los Angeles. Property was relatively cheap back then and we had plans to buy enough land to open our own artists' community. The goal was to establish it as a co-op where all the members made the decisions and shared the profits. The artists would rent their homes and studios at cost and, in turn, share their earnings with the community. Rachel was a painter and sculptress. We knew writers, musicians, and jewelry makers.

Carpentry was my bag, especially cabinet making. The new yuppies would hire me and my crew to patch their roofs or build their decks, and I'd talk them into remodeling their kitchens. I made good money, but material things didn't mean much, so we invested most of what I earned in our community. I built four small cabins and a large studio/community center. Two painters, a songwriter and a poet, were the first artists to move in. I planned a potter's shed and a glass blowing studio. The goal was for me to build more homes, and for our family to move to the community full-time as soon as our son finished middle school. We were trying to keep the disruption of his life to a minimum.

But when Jade's friend caught her mother with her father's girlfriend, something snapped. In my mind, free love had just become costly.

Rachel and I had already grown out of the open marriage, free love thing. A year earlier, we had held a ceremony on our land in which we recommitted ourselves to one another. Ten of our friends circled us holding hands, as we stood naked before them, promising we would dedicate our lives to one another, Jade and our friends.

But plans change. Our commitment ceremony, so real at the time, now seemed as quaint as bell bottoms. The greed-is-good era had replaced the Age of Aquarius. I was in business; and by God, I was going to make a buck.

I turned the hippie-dippie artists' community into condominiums. Who needed poets who read their work at local bars for drinks, and painters who sidelined as waitresses? I could get lawyers and computer geeks to pay top dollar for tiny apartments. I brought in cheap labor from Mexico and covered shabby workmanship with built-in bookcases and crown molding. The new-money crowd loved it.

Rachel complained about how I was selling out our souls, so with the help of one of my tenants, a divorce attorney, I bought her out.

Divorce wasn't difficult. Rachel and I had grown as far apart as Timothy Leary and Richard Nixon. She moved to San Francisco and I moved to Malibu. I missed Jade, but my attorney arranged generous visitation and living arrangements. I showed Jade the luxurious life that was his future while Rachel offered him the spirituality of the sixties. We co-existed for a while, perhaps even to Jade's benefit, but as he grew older he rebelled against her hippie ways. He moved in with me just before accepting a scholarship to Stanford School of Business.

I continued buying land during the recession. It's amazing how good lawyers and money can influence zoning and environmental regulations. When real estate prices boomed once again, I became rich beyond my wildest dreams. Jade majored in finance and became a successful day trader.

Now, with my third redheaded wife at my side, I sometimes wonder what happened to my values.

Then I glance at my Jag and shrug.

Brotherly Love

Paul Beckman

Dear Marshall,
It's come to my attention that you are having an affair with Betty in bookkeeping. I hacked her phone and have the lovey-dovey texts you two lovebirds have been sending each other. Enclosed is one picture of you kissing her goodnight. I have others where you both are in compromising positions. We can help each other out here—I need $100 week to pay for my son's medicine. I have no desire to share this info with your family so please mail me $100/week or $400 month and there will no longer be any reason to communicate with each other. You won't find me so don't look or your life will be one big shit storm.

To Mr. L.Phillip Revere,
It's come to my attention that you are having an affair with Betty in bookkeeping. I hacked her phone and have the lovey-dovey texts you two lovebirds have been sending each other. Enclosed is one picture of you kissing her goodnight. I have others where you both are in compromising positions. We can help each other out here—I need $100 week to pay for my son's medicine. I have no desire to share this info with your family so please mail me $100/week or $400 month and there will no longer be any reason to communicate with each other. You won't find me so don't look or your life will be one big shit storm.

Ms. Mary Goodrich- It's come to my attention that you are having an affair with Betty in bookkeeping. I hacked her phone and have the lovey-

dovey texts you two lovebirds have been sending and sexting each other. Enclosed is one picture of you kissing her goodnight. I have others where you both are in compromising positions. We can help each other out here—I need $100 per week to pay for my son's medicine. I have no desire to share this info with your family so please mail me $100/week or $400 month (a savings) and there will no longer be any reason to communicate with each other. You won't find me so don't look or your life will be one big shit storm.

"Hi Betty, how you doing?"

"I'm getting a bit confused with scheduling my three lovers in especially when they want to change days."

"Well, make it clear that you're agreeable to dropping the affair if they're unhappy."

"It's easy for you to say. You don't have to spread your legs three times a week plus extras for myself."

"Listen, Sis, we ran this scam in high school with teachers and the principal and you did okay."

"Yes but I'm getting older."

"You're 27 and hotter than you've ever been. Don't forget our deal—when you hook up with a guy or gal who wants to leave their significant other and you can quit your job and live a life of luxury we'll stop this and both have a nice little nest egg. In the meantime I want you to join Jim's Gym and we can add two or three more people to your list and since it's a private high-bucks gym you're most likely to find Mr. Money there. I'm going to boost your co-workers fees up $50 week to pay for the increase in medicine. You can drop someone every time you pick up a new lover, but that doesn't mean I'm letting them off the payoff hook."

"It seems that you're getting a little greedy and that's what got us into trouble in high school."

"Well, we're both a lot smarter now than we were in those days."

Dear Jim,

It's come to my attention that you are having an affair with Betty. I hacked her phone and have the lovey-dovey texts you two lovebirds have been sending and sexting each other. Enclosed is one picture of you kissing her goodnight. I have others where you both are in compromising positions. We can help each other out here—I need $250 per week to pay for my son's medicine. I have no desire to share this info with your family so please mail me $250/week or $1000 month (a savings) and there will no longer be any reason to communicate with each other. You won't find me so don't look or your life will be one big shit storm.

"Hi Sis, what gives and why aren't you calling on our burner phones."

"Listen, Brother, get out of town now. The game's up. Jim's family owns a spyware company and detective agency and he's got your number and is out for blood. He's sending over a couple of his Navy Seal buddies to pay you a visit."

"What about you?"

"I told him that you were blackmailing me too which pissed him off even more. Leave now. I'll find a time to get your money and send it to you. Use the classified ads to make contact when you figure out where you're moving."

"So, Betty. Did you put the fear in your brother?"

"You bet. He's gone."

"Where?"

"He'll let me know where he ends up and then I'll send him his half of the money."

"Are you serious?"

"I'm serious about sending him some money but not nearly half. After all, how can I do that when you pushed me around and cleaned out most of our savings?"

"He's bound to find out that we're a couple now and come after us."

"No way. He likes money but he hates getting beatings."

"Hi Sis. How's it going?"

"Perfect. Jim just called me from the police station and told me to get him a lawyer. Looks like you were right once again—he iced his partner five years ago and his partner's wife got incriminating evidence dropped off by a bike messenger. I'm glad I never signed a prenup."

Fake Eunuch

Robert Scotellaro

He'd been *The Mad Magician*, but his knees went out on him, so now he was doing low budget porn. As *The Mad Magician*, he had a following; did this thing in the ring where he blew a neon green powder into an opponent's face, causing them to waver helplessly in a glaze-eyed stupor. A few well-choreographed blows, and he'd have them pinned to the mat, soaking up boos from the crowd with a villain's privilege. But his knees went bad, and now it was still his bulk (particularly placed) that was keeping him gainfully employed.

The director was a woman, and she had him dressed in ancient Arabian garb, holding a long curved sword. Told him he'd be playing a eunuch guarding a harem, but he was only *pretending* to be a eunuch, and that he was a greedy bastard and would be getting it on with all of them. That it would be targeted for women. And that women liked a little story with their smut. He listened, nodded, thought, if he could be *The Mad Magician*, he could be *The Fake Eunuch*. He just hoped his knees would hold out, and the pain wouldn't take the starch out.

She introduced him to the harem, and they smiled. One of them squeezed his bicep. Another straightened his turban and said she liked his tattoos. His stage name was Rod Bigg, but his real name was Clarence Goode. He downed another pain pill when the director wasn't looking, and reminded himself not to gaze too long into the lights. The fair maidens were sprawled out on huge pillows purchased at Walmart. The sultan would be called off, and his horny bevy would grumble at the loss. Not Shakespeare, he thought.

"Okay," said the director, "that's where you come in. Hope you've been eating your Wheaties." She gave him a slap on the butt, and had the cameraman move in.

He considered his kids, the alimony payments, his apartment, and all those TV dinners and booze that weren't getting any cheaper. He tilted his turban, back the way it was. Thought, if his knees held out, even a little, he had a chance.

Goodness and Mercy

Linda Tyler

"That's funny," said Bob, pausing by the kitchen window on Saturday morning. "The car's not where you left it."

"What?" Olivia put down her bowl of cereal. She saw a dry, car-shaped patch on the wet drive, where she'd parked their red Peugeot last night.

"Funny?" said Olivia. "There's nothing funny about it. Someone's stolen the car."

She contacted the police and the insurance company to report the theft. "And we'd just had it serviced," she told them all. She slammed down the phone. "If I could lay my hands on the person who did it –"

Olivia cursed when she had to manage without the car. She didn't like travelling with 'the great unwashed'.

"It's not that bad," said Bob. "After all, I go to work on the bus."

"Hmm," said Olivia.

Visiting her friends for coffee, having lunch in town and shopping in the city were all much more difficult.

"Bob doesn't care if we don't run a car. He takes the 7.30 to work and the 5.30 home," she told her friend over lunch. "It's more difficult for me as I like to be flexible. It's cold standing outside at this time of year and when the wretched thing finally arrives it's full of smelly wet people fogging up the windows. Besides, standing at a bus stop is humiliating."

"It must be," her friend said, sipping a glass of chardonnay. "Why not get a taxi?"

"Bob says we can't afford it with all the money I spend. He's such a skinflint." Olivia stroked her pearl necklace. "I bought this last week, but did he appreciate what a bargain I got?"

Her friend tutted.

Pleased, Olivia forked up the remains of her smoked salmon.

Olivia climbed off the bus, trudged down the road and stopped dead. Outside the house was the red Peugeot.

She inspected the car. Clean and newly-polished, it had obviously been looked after during its little excursion. Not even a broken window.

Then she saw tucked under the windscreen wiper a brown envelope. '*To whom it may concern*' was written on it. With shaking fingers, she tore open the envelope.

'*Sorry*,' it said in the same confident hand. '*I borrowed your car when I lost my wallet and didn't have enough money to get home. Please accept the enclosed as a token of my remorse.*'

Olivia peered inside the envelope. Tickets for next Friday night's screening of the latest James Bond.

"You know how expensive that cinema is," she said to Bob once inside the house. "And the best seats."

Again she contacted the police and the insurance company, this time to report the car's reappearance. The young police officer came and took another statement. "It's amazing what you can do with a piece of wire," he said, and told her she was lucky – most cars were taken by joy-riders and ended up abandoned wrecks. Olivia didn't tell him about the free tickets; that was none of his business.

"I'll arrange for the car to be taken away for analysis," he said. "We'll get it back to you as soon as possible."

"Why can't you do it here?" she demanded.

"It has to be fingerprinted by Crime Scene Investigation," he told her.

"CSI?" said Bob, after the officer had left. "That sounds exciting."

"Oh, for goodness sake," said Olivia. "And that policeman is far too young."

"The police obviously have no idea how inconvenient all this is," she said to her friend at their weekly lunch date. "I warned them not to damage the car."

Her friend nodded. "You have to keep them on their toes these days."

"I'm not wearing my fur coat on public transport," she told Bob.

But the Peugeot was returned by the evening of the film.

"No prints," the officer said. "The thief must have worn gloves. He clearly knew what he was doing."

"Of course he wore gloves," said Olivia. "I would have thought you of all people would know that."

They drove into town and Bob parked in a well-lit street.

"I hope the car's here when we get back," Olivia sniffed.

They enjoyed the film and celebrated their good fortune by going for a meal afterwards. By the time they arrived home, it was late. Olivia noticed the front door, half-hidden in leafy shadows, didn't look right. Then she realised – it was standing ajar.

"Bob," she hissed. "Look."

With a sudden jolt, Olivia remembered the spare house key she always kept in the car. She wrenched open the glove compartment, scrabbling through the bits of paperwork. The key wasn't there.

She put her hand to her neck. Thank goodness she was wearing the pearl necklace that was such a bargain. But –

"Wait here," said Bob. "It might not be safe to go in."

He crept up the path and pushed tentatively on the door.

"Hello?" he called.

"Never mind that," said Olivia, brushing past him.

"Heaven help you if you're still here!" she shouted. Snatching up the umbrella from the hallstand, she stormed through the house.

"Perhaps we forgot to lock the door behind us when we went out," said Bob, following at a trot behind.

"Don't talk wet," she said.

She moved through the house, switching on lights as she went. The state-of-the-art TV in the sitting-room, the laptop in the dining-room, Bob's hand-made model of the Flying Scotsman in his study were all still in place.

Olivia climbed the stairs, her mouth fixed in a grimace. In their bedroom, wardrobe doors and chest drawers gaped open, their contents strewn over the floor.

The designer handbag she hadn't yet unwrapped, the shiny leather boots she was saving to wear at the next lunch with her friends, her Louis Vuitton suitcase – gone.

She saw propped up on the dressing-table a plain white card covered in familiar writing. '*Glad you were able to make use of the tickets and hope you enjoyed the film. I've certainly had an excellent evening.*'

Place Your Bets

Jim Bell

Breaking News: Diamond State Politics

Sports Betting Finally Arrives

Updated 2:30 PM
Posted 7:05 AM
By Larry Stillwell
Diamond Advance Media for diamond.com

Gentlemen, Place Your Bets!

After years of anticipation, legal sports betting has become a reality in the Diamond State. In a landmark decision, the courts ruled in favor of the state's argument that the federal ban on sports betting, enacted in the early '90s, was unconstitutional.

"This is fantastic news for everyone in the Diamond State," Governor Todd Jenkins told reporters gathered for the announcement at the Stonegate racetrack. "This is the culmination of a decades-long effort to bring legal sports betting to our great state. Americans spend billions of dollars each year on sports betting through illegal bookies. We want in on a piece of the action."

Millions of taxpayer dollars have been spent over the years on lobbying efforts and court battles to overturn the ban. When asked to comment, the governor replied, "Isn't it wonderful that our citizens now have an opportunity to recoup those losses by placing a bet or two. We want to make betting accessible to more people in our state, particularly the disenfranchised who have limited opportunities for upward mobility. We are now providing hopes and dreams to those among us who have little hope and virtually no dreams."

Lucky Lou Gianncano, the noted bookmaker and the state's partner in securing influence for the decision, echoed the governor's endorsement. "I've been in this business a lotta years, long before anybody thought about legalizing any of it. I can tell you, everybody's looking to get rich quick and sports betting is a great way for them to play the odds." The governor nodded enthusiastically in agreement.

The ruling will allow people to place bets on games in professional and college sports, a move that many of the nations teams and owners feel will hurt the public's view of their games.

"I, along with many owners and team management, am concerned that this ruling will tarnish the image of sports. People will no longer think of sports as a beautiful display of athleticism and professionalism. They might come to view sports as a money-making machine driven by pure greed," said Don Billet, owner of the Power City Sparkplugs when reached at his island retreat.

Governor Jenkins highlighted the economic benefits of sports betting to the state. "Our hope is the betting activity will generate millions of dollars to boost the state's casino and horse-racing industries, which have been struggling for years. We're gambling that we will finally have a form of betting that will pay off for our state. If we can get more people hooked on betting, it should spread to other forms of gambling as well."

To kick off the grand event, the governor had the honor of placing the first bet. When asked where he would wager, Jenkins replied, "I'm torn. I'm an avid fan of baseball, but there's something about the allure of a good cage match. It's growing in popularity and it offers tremendous potential for the betting industry. That's where I'm going to put my money."

Small Sweet Thing

Alex Reece Abbott

Your grandmother holds out an old blue biscuit tin. On crisp, white baking paper you spy small, even, golden morsels; breathe sweet vanilla.

Mama's little baby loves shortenin', shortenin', Mama's little baby loves shortenin' bread...

She sings to you – maybe you're three? – smearing butter on a little round cake, then fills your cupped palm with warmth. Your mouth waters. You devour her gift. And smile. With your entire being, you know you are blessed.

Years on, you puzzle why, at the furthest edge of the Empire, your Irish migrant grandmother sings you a Plantation song. And, why she sings about shortbread, when you're eating a pikelet.

Then you learn that the song was a hit, written by a populist American poet, around the turn of the last century.

You read that shortening bread is a mix of corn meal, flour, hot water, eggs, baking powder, milk and shortening; a fried batter bread. Not shortbread. And you find out that pikelets are also known as the 'poor man's crumpet'. People who could not afford rings to make crumpets would fry the batter, dropping it freely into the pan.

Last week, you discovered that your grandmother worked in the kitchen of Currygrane, a *teach mór*, one of the Anglo-Irish big houses. You see her, standing at the huge, blackened wood range, a girl flipping pikelets on a heavy griddle.

They call them Scotch Pancakes here. From the Welsh – *bara piglydd*, we call them pikelets. The perfect word for a warm, buttery, bite-sized morsel of love.

You have a pikelet recipe packed away... somewhere. It's not her recipe.

In a virtual old blue biscuit tin, you have the memory packed away... in crisp, white baking paper, safe for now. You devour it on special occasions.

Your small, sweet pikelet.

The Sugar Assassin

Jo Davies

I commit my crime openly, but no court in the land would convict me. Instead I get praise; told how *nice* I am. Fools.

It wasn't always so. At first, I tried to help; to teach them a better way. I used to create nutritious, nourishing food for work celebrations, but my efforts were snubbed in favour of cheap, supermarket fodder. Next to the chocolate-smothered, plastic sponge cake and factory-made cookies, my homemade sugar-free coconut bites went untouched.

Then, one morning, I was pushed too far by an aggressive colleague. An aggressive colleague with a well-known weakness: greed. That afternoon there was a team celebration – our boss brought in cakes. And there, in the office, an idea was born.

"Here, have mine," I passed the plate of sugary jam doughnuts to my aggressor with a smile.

"Oh go on then," she laughed as her fat fingers grasped a second cake.

I watched her take big bites of the soft dough, savouring the knowledge that a massive surge of insulin was that very second pumping from her over-worked pancreas. The sugar would suppress her immune system for at least 24 hours. I wondered how strongly the gluten-derived exorphins would affect her brain, giving her a mild feeling of euphoria, strengthening her addiction to wheat and increasing her chances of cancer, dementia, diabetes and a whole host of other diseases.

After that watershed moment, I dusted off my old recipe book and went back to baking the old-fashioned way.

My generous donations of sugary creations go to those I despise the most – those deceitful colleagues whose insatiable greed for power sees them manipulate and trample the rest of us in their selfish pursuit of glory. My gooey chocolate brownies have gained legendary status, while my moist carrot cake has a strong following amongst those who fancy themselves more 'health-conscious'. Idiots.

It helps me cope with my more difficult colleagues to know that, with every bite, this anti-nutrient 'food' is surely storing up future health problems. Not only do my victims welcome their poison with open arms, they become more amenable, even grateful.

Some might eventually die from avoidable health problems; many will suffer pain and inflammatory illnesses, while others will simply fade into the tight embrace of dementia. I'm not fussed which way it goes really.

I'm poisoning them, but no court in the land would convict me.

The Booth

Andrew Grenfell

Entering the club is another world, a world of *Lest we forget*, Keno, Sunday's roast lunch special, luridly patterned carpet, winning ticket wins a meat tray, and Dad in a thick grey cardigan much too musty even for here, so I walk on cautious footsteps to where he sits, hunched over, twisted hands stubbornly clutching the buttons, and inevitably the endless flashing lights and bleep and bloop of the machines sends reeling back that imprinted image in my mind: this man trapped in a glass cage of his own greed, a trap of striving for what he could never quite reach, grasping at something more than disappointment, more than regret, more than grinding away day after day, a shortcut, a day that was supposed to be the best day of my dad's life, but became the worst.

    He would sit at the kitchen table, filling out entries for competitions, laboriously writing out the addresses on heavy cream envelopes, sealing them up, half a dozen at a time deposited into the post-box down our street, never entrusting anyone else with the posting, begrudgingly letting us walk there with him, a kind of shuffling hope in that stride, the clear morning throwing sharp shadows across the pavement, and then the ritual feeding of the letters one by one, gulped up by the dark gullet of the red box.

    Congratulations, my mother read aloud to us, after Dad passed over the typed letter to her, his eyes shining. *You have been chosen*. It was as if we had all won; as if, after all those years of dispensing hope into small square parcels, we were seeing our luck turn around.

The fateful day drew nearer, Dad as excited and happy as we had ever seen him (which is to say, less brooding and taciturn than usual, fewer mysterious late night disappearances, less silent glowering at us with his hoary breath, his shaggy jet-black hair merging with the darkness) and we even had an outing to the other side of town, where we visited a family we knew from our camping holidays, the Carlsens, who lived in an impossibly big house with an outdoor spa pool that commanded a view of the twinkling city skyline that muted us with intimidation.

The four of us kids knew Dad still wouldn't say much on the ride to the TV station, but we couldn't help pestering him with questions anyway: *How long will it go for? What type of notes will it be, mostly? Do you have a whatsit, a strategy, Dad?* He grunted now and again in response, but there were twinkles around the corners of his eyes; and I imagined, as our car bumped along that unfamiliar street, my ten-year-old mind unburdened by the weight of adulthood, of unrealistic expectation, in that moment where anything seeming possible, having a dad who chatted nonchalantly about sport, or gossiped about celebrities, or posed thorny scientific questions – anything, really, but his relentless silence – and who gave his children a proper big hug before bed like the Carlsens seemed to do.

We bundled into the studio, colourful lights and sounds like the pokie machine rooms that my Dad frequented (and we were only allowed to glimpse) on a grand scale, and in the middle of it, the transparent man-sized cylindrical booth where Dad would meet his destiny: 'The Great Cash Grab' blinked the display, and out came our father in his best slacks and collared shirt from the wings of the studio, bright lights in his eyes, a forced grin on his face.

Cameras rolled and Dad climbed in. The countdown began.

It fell to zero and then started again at 60, banknotes roiling wildly in the cylinder, blown by powerful jets at its base, a whirlwind of money whipping around him, and his arms, his hands, clawing and pawing, clutching in the pulsing light, a frivolous melody playing over the speakers – *it was rigged against me*, he would say later, justifying it to himself as much as to us, *you couldn't see a damn thing* – and later, the final salt in the wound, Dad having to front up for publicity photographs holding up his meagre haul, a mere fistful of 5s and 10s, which could not have totalled more than two hundred dollars.

These many years later that day still seems fresh and clear to me: the day our family was riven in two, my Dad never the same, retreating into his special brand of sullen anger, my mother becoming withdrawn into herself, all of us kids learning to shelter ourselves from the gusts of his moods; Dad the breadwinner, Dad spending money only on himself (drink, cigarettes, gambling), Dad leaving a puny weekly allowance for Mum, Dad reserving his rare good moods for his mates at the pub, spurred by a drink or four or six, none of it seeming real any more when I now try to trace the threads of our lives in my Dad's weathered face in the RSL, the lights of poker machines dancing on the surface of his rheumy eyes, etching shadowy lines on his cheeks, on the careless stubble on his chin, illuminating a cigarette turning itself to ash near his busy fingers, slippery light running away into hidden corners, like everything I can't say to him: that perversely I want to thank him, for the example he gave to me, for unwittingly making me financially prudent, for being the reason that I hug my kids, for nurturing a well of love growing up that can only now be expended.

Yes, I tell myself before I catch his eye, I do want to thank him, for everything he didn't give us, that made us rich.

Lieberman

Larry Lefkowitz

Lieberman was found at home slumped over his writing desk, dead. He was a literary critic. It was said of him that he had more rivals who wished him gone than did an organized crime boss. His 'colleague', Kunzman – colleague in a professional sense only (in actuality, he was, hierarchically, the second critic after chief critic Lieberman) was notified of Lieberman's death by Grossman from the print shop. "He probably pricked himself accidentally with his poison pen," Grossman said. The cautious Kunzman allowed himself an acknowledging nod; he could afford to do so, Grossman being a firm non-admirer of Lieberman due to the latter's penchant for last minute printing changes when the literary review he ran with an iron hand was about to go to press.

There popped into Kunzman's thoughts, perhaps in contrition at his failure to murmur something in Lieberman's defense in the face of Grossman's barb, the final words – worthy of an obituary, if not Lieberman's – of Thomas Mann's 'Death in Venice': "And before nightfall a shocked and respectful world received the news of his decease." No, not Lieberman's death. Shocked, maybe. Respectful, but few. Ashenbach had his failures, but they were not those of a literary critic.

As assistant critic to Lieberman, Kunzman was called upon to write Lieberman's obituary. Possibilities danced in his head.

"The grand old man of literary criticism"? "Grand" didn't fit. "Grand curmudgeon" might do. Or maybe a reference to Lieberman's "curmudgeonic pen" would be sufficient.

On more than one occasion, Kunzman had had the desire to murder Lieberman. There was the time that Lieberman had stolen from Kunzman's brilliant review of a novel by A.B. Yehoshua, which review he had left on his desk, and which Lieberman, as was his wont, had "blatantly seized with his prehensile hands" (according to the condemnatory phrase that Kunzman uttered only to himself so long as Lieberman had been among the living), read it, and published it with a minimum of changes under his own name, including Kunzman's most honed metaphors. Lieberman ruled 'his' review with an iron pen. After all, there were readers who purchased the literary review principally in order to read Lieberman's reviews in it, particularly delighting in his scathing ones, in which he heaped fire and brimstone with the generosity of one of Satan's helpers.

His writing a malicious obituary for Lieberman would have been easy. "We could hear him before we could see him – his grumblings, his shouts, sometimes his belches." At such times, Kunzman would curse him (under his breath, of course, unless Lieberman was beyond earshot, then Kunzman would say to his secretary, "Saul is in full bloom"). Kunzman would have titled his obituary, "Death of a *Gegner*" ("Againstnik", in Yiddish). Or he could apply to Lieberman Churchill's words about himself, that he was "so conceited that he could not believe the gods would create so potent a being as him for so prosaic an ending." But the traditional Jewish injunction against speaking ill of the dead stayed his hand.

And, thought Kunzman, if I had gone first, I could imagine Lieberman's obituary homage to me. He would write: "It was I who first noticed Kunzman's great talent. I who gave him his first job, I who nurtured his art," and so forth. I would have had to come back from the dead to ask him, "Excuse me, but who died, you or I?" And how had Lieberman first noticed his great talent – the first thing Kunzman wrote for him elicited the response: "I could write better with my *tuchas*." Other times, Lieberman adopted a more subtle approach, which he had apparently taken from the Japanese Handbook of Literary Rejection. He would return a review to Kunzman, or to someone else, with a written note to the effect that "the review was so magnificently written that it would be a travesty to print it in a literary journal so pedestrian as our own. Therefore, I feel compelled to return the scintillating piece with gratitude and a deep bow, and I will never forget the glorious experience of reading such an extraordinary work." Because of the feeling that it produced in the recipient, it became known as a '*seppuku* rejection'.

Whichever form of rejection Lieberman chose, Kunzman mused, it was his way to knock you down in order to raise you up so that you would be grateful when he didn't criticize you, or throw you a crumb of half-praise – albeit that even in the latter event you couldn't be sure he wasn't being ironic. Well, Kunzman sighed, now Lieberman was gone, at least freed at last from the need to search out metaphors, or to 'borrow' them from Kunzman. And not only metaphors – great swathes of material. Once, apparently seeing the frustration on Kunzman's face after a particularly egregious lifting, Lieberman quoted Tennyson: "It is the unimaginative man who thinks everything borrowed." Should have been Lieberman's epitaph, thought Kunzman ruefully.

* * *

In the end, Kunzman felt that he had settled his score with Lieberman by penning an obituary which was an encomium-anti-encomium, an obituary which damned with faint praise, particularly by his utilizing the "Fall of a Titan" title to allow him to insert in the body of the obituary a carefully wrought obfuscating, serpentine paragraph-length sentence, an extended simile of the Titanic sinking in such a way as to suggest that Lieberman sometimes behaved in a literarily disastrous manner. He only hoped that in a corner of the world on high (or low) Lieberman wasn't waiting for him. Lieberman was not one for leaving accounts unsettled.

Kunzman would go to the funeral, of course, and would force back any threatening-to-surface gleeful urges centered around the thought that now he would be the literary review's chief critic.

An Exceptional Young Whine

Peter Lingard

Jimmy Winter whined, which is why we called him Whiner. We weren't masters of the Queen's English, my mates and me. (Should that be I?) We lazily eased his name from Winter to Winner (tees were too hard), before arriving at Whiner. Of course, he never said a word about being called Winner. His mother wasn't ecstatic, but, after a few half-hearted attempts to get us to pronounce their family name correctly, she let it drop. You would, wouldn't you? "Hey, this is Jimmy Winner." However, like I said, it was only a short time before we arrived at Whiner. He didn't even mind that name. He'd discovered early that when he whined, he usually got what he wanted. We had him whine to his father for two sets of wickets so we could play cricket. It only took him a day! He started whining on Saturday and on Sunday his father gave in. He drove Jimmy to the store and purchased wickets, a bat and a ball. Winner! We only had a couple of badly dinged bats and a tennis ball before that, so the Winter donation was much appreciated. Jimmy didn't really like cricket but we'd go to the Winters' side door and ask if he could come out to play, with his gear of course. When we got to the park, he'd sit and watch. After a while, he'd get bored and start whining about it. We'd relent and let him bat, bowling underarm to him, just so he wouldn't decide to go home and take his wickets with him. It didn't occur to us then that we were pandering to his whining.

To be honest, he didn't whine much when around us because we wouldn't put up with it, unless we needed something. He figured out being silent was preferable to being punched. He didn't whine to girls, either. In fact, the only people we knew he whined to were his parents.

Girls liked him a lot, and they shared stuff with him. He got them so well organised they brought refreshments to our games: quartered oranges, sliced carrots and cucumbers, and lollies. Then Celia, a girl I admired, said we should get a baseball bat and mitt. Jimmy whined his dad up and the items appeared soon after. Only then did Celia reveal her cunning plan; we should let the girls play with us. Baseball, she said, was nothing more than a glorified game of rounders. We could make up teams of both girls and boys. For a sweetener, she suggested that if we supplied the makings, the girls would cook us all some hot dogs with fried onions at one of the park's barbeques. It was a difficult step to take but Jimmy liked the idea and pointed out that if we wanted to acquire more stuff from his folks, we should let the girls play. At Celia's suggestion, Jimmy whined up his mum for the dogs and onions and we all enjoyed four games and two sausages the following Saturday. When Celia asked if we played field hockey, I told her she was reaching too far.

When footy season arrived, I asked Dad if he would get me a new football. He said I should add it to my Christmas or birthday list. My birthday is in January, so I convinced Jimmy to whine up his father again. The man didn't even try to stall; he just went to the store and returned with two spanking balls. Winner! I asked Celia if she and her friends wanted to become our cheerleaders but she gave me a look of disdain. I said we could get Jimmy to whine outfits out of his mum but she wasn't impressed. I'd known it was a long shot. Jimmy whined for a couple of rugby balls but his mother forbade her husband to buy them.

Come August, there was a pause between our sports seasons and I wondered what we could get Jimmy to whine up for us. I'd watched the Olympics on the telly and fantasised of my anticipated prowess with a javelin, but Celia said I was getting greedy and, besides, it was far too dangerous. I'd also enjoyed equestrian events, especially the cross country. Celia laughed and said, "Good luck with that."

I saw her words as a challenge. "Jimmy," I said. "I need you to whine…"

Nothing in This Truck is Worth Dying for

Jonathan Slusher

I bit off a corner of the pill and nearly spat it into the sink before I remembered. Down the drain was no good. Supposedly fish around the world were being found with trace levels of Prozac in their system. That was crazy. I aimed for the trash can instead. Besides, I was almost done with that stuff for good. This time was going to be different. The stinging chatter in my mind had quieted down to a soft whisper, but I wanted more. That was my new mantra. It wasn't greedy to want to take up more space in the world again. I was going to try to be more assertive with my choices and worry less about making them.

Things went smoothly for a while.

Eventually I made a bad call. It was bound to happen sooner or later. I should have stayed on the freeway, but traffic was backed up everywhere. There was no chance of being on time now. It must have been an accident. Everyone was screwed. No one was going anywhere for a while.

But suddenly in the rearview a silver jacked up F250 pickup appeared and tore down the shoulder lane. It sped past hundreds of backed up cars. The truck nosed itself in front of the car in front of me.

That wasn't fair! I reminded myself that I wasn't in New Jersey anymore. This was Northern California. People took the high road here. People were better than that. No one beeped or yelled profanities at aggressive jerks on the road. It didn't ever do any good to let the haters get you all bent out of shape.

Traffic crawled along and the pickup merged into the left lane. It had a bumper sticker with black block text on a white background.

Nothing in this Truck is Worth Dying for

What a dumbass! I shook my head and held it in.

A deep bass thumped through the truck's custom sound speakers, it wasn't 'Cat Scratch Fever' but it might as well have been Ted Nugent himself at the wheel. Everything about this guy sucked.

There was a MAGA sticker and a Terrorist Hunting Permit on the truck's rear window. Of course the driver was soft and out of shape. If he were dropped in the desert with a backpack and a heavy assault rifle to hunt terrorists he wouldn't last two days.

The truck was a diesel. It had giant chrome wheels without a speck of dirt. Perhaps not everyone who drove like a fool in a squeaky clean mini monster truck was overcompensating for male insecurity. I was certain that this guy was. Passive aggressive provocateurs seemed to be taking over the county.

Try to remain objective and open minded and optimistic. He was the broken one not me. I reminded myself to feel bad for him. He probably didn't even have a girlfriend. Trolls must live sad existences.

Soon our windows were side by side. I stared at the driver incredulously, but he wouldn't look over. His false careless sneer focused straight ahead.

My window was already rolled down and I wanted to yell, "Hey! Someone put a stupid bumper sticker on your truck. They must be playing a joke on you."

I held back. It should have felt good to be the bigger man, but it didn't.

Traffic crawled along. At the next intersection, the truck turned left.

I wanted to follow him and give him the finger.

I wanted to sarcastically yell, "Lock her Up!" and "Make America Great Again!"

I wanted to drag him out of window by his hair and let him know that my dad had been killed in a hit and run accident with a jacked up F250 pickup when I was nine years old.

Dad had been a Marine Sergeant.

It didn't seem fair to hold it all in while the small-minded, insecure shitheads careened around the country unchecked and unchallenged. Dad wouldn't have put up with it. Dad would have let people know how angry he was. Dad would have done something.

Dad wouldn't need any pills.

The next morning I bit off a slightly bigger piece and spat it out in the trash.

Boom or Bust

Irene Buckler

As his finances crash, his dander rises.

"You know what that is, Mr Money Bags?" he fumes. "It's avarice, sheer greed!"

What can I say? I admit that I have been lucky, but we are all playing by the same set of rules. While I have been steadily building up my bank balance and managing my property portfolio, he has been in and out of prison. Now he cannot pay his rent.

"There must be something you can do," she pleads on his behalf. "He is facing ruin. If he sells that house to you, he will have lost his only source of income."

She should talk. After outrageously overcommitting herself, she has had to offload the bulk of her assets, too. I was able to purchase them from her at a bargain basement price and now it's his turn. Soon I will take ownership of everything they have. Business is business.

"If you can't pay me," I remind him, calmly facing him down, "then you have no choice but to declare yourself bankrupt."

Enraged, he upturns the table and storms out of the room.

"I did try to warn you, dear," Mum says as we crawl around picking up the pieces and I have to admit she is right.

Dad doesn't know how to lose a game of Monopoly with any dignity.

Enemies

Joe Mills

Gary's team stunk last year, and already during the practices it had been clear they were going to stink this year. Trey had only signed his son up because it would have looked bad if his kid wasn't on the company team. Otherwise he would never have put him on a co-ed team, something that woman from … Accounting? Marketing? Customer Service? … had made a big deal about. We wouldn't put together a Whites Only team would we? Any team MAC sponsored had to be open to all. We don't discriminate against our members, and we can't sponsor a team that does. She had pre-empted the idea of two separate teams before anyone had suggested it.

That woman had also wanted the MAC team name changed from Pirates to something less aggressive. Pirates were rapists and murderers. She had suggested Ducks for god's sake. If she had used Oregon as an example, people might have listened, but she didn't know anything about sports or any actual teams. Instead she had gone on and on about how impressive ducks were. How they were amphibious and had the ability to swim, walk, and fly. How they were role models and animal totems. How that's what we wanted to teach the children. The ability to adapt to diverse environments. She wouldn't fucking shut up. There's always one who takes over a meeting. You just have to wait them out. Without talking, without moving. That just encourages them. You have to wait motionless, like a snake. Trey had been concerned because a few people had been nodding as if they agreed. Some will agree to any dipshit thing. Then there are those who nod because they think it makes them look like they're listening and will protect them. He should have suggested the Nodders as a team name. The Go-Alongs. He wanted to say, Ducks? Ducks get eaten. Ducks get shot. You want to know why MAC got taken over? Because we're ducks. We wanted to do a bunch of different things, walk, dive, fly, and we didn't do any of them very well, and we got swallowed by a predator that did one thing very very well. Eat the weak. They ate us, and they're going to shit us out.

It's like these handshakes between teams before the game. What's that about? Afterwards, fine, that's tradition, but right now, that other team is the enemy. That's the way it worked. A month ago, those kids might have been teammates, even friends, but once the rosters were set, it became "us" and "them." *They* cheat. *They* push. *They* don't play fair. *They* are jerks. *They* are the enemy, whoever they are. That's the way it is, and that's the way it should be. Sports isn't about character and feel-good bullshit; it is about competition, and it is about competition making you strong.

The problem right now is the enemy isn't the other team, it is Gary's own team. It is people who want to be ducks or who want his kid to be a duck. Look at the bleachers. Look at where most of them are. Sitting on the bottom and in the middle. Why doesn't everyone try to sit at the top? Maybe the fat ones and handicapped collapse at the first rows, but who starts up the steps and stops halfway? What's the point? You go to the top or you don't go. It's not like these are nose-bleed seats here. The problem is the fucking nodders and middlers. They do the minimum, and they teach their kids to do the minimum. Just run half-speed. Just do part of the drills. Coach asks for five pushups? Pretend to do two, laughing. And Gary has to play with the kids of these lazy-asses. These fucking duck-wannabes.

It doesn't matter now, playing for the company team. Looking like a team member. Not with the takeover. He should move Gary to a different league. Maybe get him on one of the Spanish teams they see at the other parks. They are disciplined. They are aggressive. They probably celebrate victories with slabs of meat instead of juice boxes and Sun Chips. Their name sure as hell wouldn't be *pollo* or whatever duck is in Spanish. They would be Toros or Perros Locos. That's what his son needs. Plus he'd learn Spanish. Real Spanish. Not classroom Spanish. Not "Hello, how are you? My name is Gary. Please beat me up." But useful, fuck-your-mother Spanish.

That is where the new markets are. Maybe if some of them spoke Spanish, there would still be a MAC. A couple years ago, there had been a few Hispanics kicking the ball around, then they had a team, and now they had their own league. Who was selling to them? MAC hadn't been. They were their own enemy. They weren't paying attention; they had been paddling around in circles, and got swept over the falls. Dead ducks.

Gary shouldn't play soccer at all. A sport that handicapped him? That taught him not to use his hands? It gives him the wrong idea. It makes him accept being limited. Too many people do that already. Not letting them use what they had. The PC and the prejudiced. The rules and regulations. They should be allowed to run and play any way they want. Hands. Head. Feet. Fucking Mixed Martial Arts ball.

He should have Gary switch sports. Soccer wouldn't prepare him. Trey could see it already with the merger, and that hadn't even been radical change. That had just been run-of-the-mill business. It was nothing compared to what was coming. If scientists were right, and he wasn't one of those deniers, the earth was warming up, the polar ice caps were melting, and the oceans would rise. Ten feet. Fifty feet. After a couple feet, it didn't matter how much. Coastlines everywhere would change

Gary was lucky. Right now, all the beaches and good coastal real estate have been developed, but a reset was coming. The board was going to be cleaned. The Etch-a-Sketch was going to be shaken. It was going to be a chance for Gary's generation. There would be fortunes to be made. Not for Trey, he was too old. He'd had the misfortune to be born in an era of stability. No massive World Wars. The wars in his time hadn't been big enough, transformative enough. But Gary? God, the opportunities he was going to have. The world was changing. Tipping points all over the place. Gary was going to have chances that he never did. He just had to be ready and be tough. He had to know who his enemies were, and that was everyone.

Haunting Our Hearts and Pocketbook

Meryl Baer

"Toast, he's the color of toast," and ten-year-old Jason christened our new kitten because of the light brown splotches dotting his white fur.

Toast became a spoiled member of the family, demanding food, water and hugs, and forbidding other animals from entering his domain. Visiting dogs remained outside or confined to one room. Toast had the run of the house, although he quickly grew into a less energetic cat with a few extra pounds around the middle.

Our favorite feline disliked cold weather and during snowstorms shunned the outdoors. Waddling over to the back door, staring expectantly at the closest human, someone obediently opened the door for him. Stretching his neck out, slowly moving his head back and forth while carefully observing the white landscape, he would turn, stare at us and scurry back inside. Too cold, too snowy, too wet for this prima donna.

Later he would walk to the front door, whining to go out NOW, and somebody obliged. Opening the door to let him out, once again he eagerly took a couple of steps across the threshold, scanned the scene and ran inside again, throwing his owners a disgusted look. It was not our fault the weather was lousy in both the front and back of the house.

In good weather Toast donned his hunting persona, skulked outdoors and triumphantly returned with a bird or two, so proud of himself!

Toast grew older, wider and heavier. The years rolled by and Jason and his brother Matthew grew up, tall and slim, and left town. It was time to downsize, the house too big for two adults and one cat.

The For Sale sign went up in front of the house months before our next home, a new townhouse, was finished. We did not expect to sell immediately. The realtor warned us the area was experiencing a slow real estate market.

The house listed only a few days when the realtor brought a young family around. They toured and left. A few days later they returned, carefully inspecting each room once again. They fell in love with the house, made an offer, and wanted to move in quickly.

Unwilling to allow the sale to fall through, not knowing when and if the next offer might come along, we opted to rent until our new home was ready.

I did not realize how difficult it would be finding a temporary apartment that accepted pets, but after numerous frustrating phone calls found a small one bedroom. The apartment complex charged a pet penalty, $50 more per month than the quoted rental price for the privilege of accommodating Toast.

We signed the rental agreement and prepared to relocate, selling stuff, giving things to the boys, and placing boxes of prized possessions and furniture in storage until the final move.

The hectic last week at home entailed packing, cleaning, transporting belongings to the apartment, finalizing the house closing, meanwhile working every day.

Poor Toast had no idea what was going on. We explained the situation to him, telling him he would love his new home, but the old cat was losing his hearing and mental acuity and did not understand. His body rebelled against the changes swirling around him, becoming lethargic, which is saying a lot. A mature cat of 13 years, he spent most of the time sleeping and wandering sluggishly around the house, occasionally venturing outdoors, staying close to beloved, familiar surroundings.

Toast was no longer eating. It was time to take him to the vet.

The vet diagnosed some disorder and explained, "Toast needs to take one of these pills three times a day. He probably won't cooperate. One person needs to hold his mouth open while someone else places the pill as far down his throat as possible. If it's not far enough down he will spit it out."

Toast was not cooperative, howling and obstinate as his tired, old body actively fought attempts to force the pills into his mouth.

He did not improve.

It was as if he was telling us, "I've had it. It's been fun, but Jason and Matthew no longer live here and you two run around all the time and I am lonely and tired. Let's face it, the boys were much more fun than you guys. And what's all this about taking away my furniture and favorite possessions? I do not even recognize this barren place anymore!"

On moving day Toast refused to budge. Steve took him to the vet one more time. A couple of hours later he walked into my office and shared the bad news. "There wasn't much of a choice. I didn't want to prolong his agony. Toast is in cat heaven."

I was sad, but knew it was for the best. Old and tired, unwilling to relocate and adjust to a new place, we would move without him.

That evening we spent our first night in our temporary residence. It was missing something – the comfort of our precious Toast.

Unfortunately the apartment management company was not comforting, consoling or caring, obliging us to pay the $50 monthly animal fee every month while living in the apartment. "Greedy bitches," Steve griped.

Toast lived on in our hearts and pocketbook.

Catch a Tiger

Cynthia Leslie-Bole

I found it in his wallet. As far as I knew, Douglas had never been out of the country; hell, he had supposedly never been out of Pennsylvania, but there it was, carefully folded inside a small white envelope with his name written in flowery script on the outside. Douglas had always been a private one. He'd tell people he kept his cards close to his chest and his lips zipped. Well, that may be fine and dandy in business, or in international espionage, but in a marriage? Not so much.

When I first met Douglas at Izzy's Bar, his reticence gave him the allure of mystery. As we dated, our quiet walks made me wonder even more what made the man tick. He'd stare out at the green fringe of woods, shutting me out of his inner world, and I wanted nothing more than to penetrate his facade and glimpse the real Douglas waiting to be brought into the light by me, only by me. I wanted him. I wanted his secrets. I was sure they were more compelling than mine.

So I was patient. I asked questions just probing enough to glean information but never invasive enough to send him running. I snooped around asking what people knew about him. And he told me a little here and there until I got to know the skeletal details of his life with five sisters, a ferret, and an alcoholic mother. I knew where he went to high school, how he flubbed his football career, even that his first love at 16 was named Belinda.

When I got him to marry me—and let me tell you, that took some doing—I knew his job history, what he liked for dinner, and how he liked to make love, but when I complained that he never let me really know him, he'd mumble something illuminating like, "What you see is what you get."

So when he started getting even more distant, working more hours at the World Market where he managed imports, I resolved to get answers and do a bit more sleuthing. Didn't find out anything much, but it gave me something to do other than wait for him to show up for dinner. I knew the contents of his drawers and his side of the closet: nothing revealing at all. I even read through a thin stack of letters from his mother and scanned his email and text messages, but he remained opaque as oatmeal. That made me even more determined to beat him at his own game.

So yeah, maybe I was wrong to go into his wallet one Sunday, but ya gotta know who the hell you're married to, don't you?

When I saw that small envelope, my heart jumped. It felt like I was finally about to flush him out of hiding and beat him at his own game. And then I opened the envelope and saw a multicolored piece of foreign currency inside. I pulled it out and was electrified by the sexy danger of the tiger on the back. Its mouth was open with white fangs and a blood-red tongue visible. I could almost smell its musk and feel its meaty breath. Behind the tiger stood an elephant with a raised trunk and crazy squiggles of some unrecognizable language. At least unrecognizable to me, but who knows what it might have said to Douglas? Perhaps he could speak the language fluently, perhaps all his best friends traded in this currency, perhaps he was a tiger tamer and an elephant rider. How the hell was I to know?

When I flipped the bill, I saw the words Reserve Bank of

India and Gandhi's childlike grin, mocking me with its innocence.

Well, well, I thought, what have we here? To my knowledge, not one single Indian lived in Oil City, PA, so where the hell did the bill come from? Who had written Douglas' name on the envelope with such feminine artistry?

When he finally came in from mowing the lawn, I presented roast beef and mashed potatoes with a few unthreatening green beans thrown in for vitamins. I even poured him a beer after having harped about how he should lose weight if he wanted to live to see forty. Then I brought it up, unskillfully, I admit.

"So, Doug-Man," (he hated when I called him that), "how is diversity at World Market these days? Do you have any minority employees at the store?"

"Nope," was his response.

"Hmm, do you even know any minorities, like Mexicans or Koreans or Indians?"

"Nope," he said shoveling potatoes into his shuttered face.

"Then why do you have a ten rupee note in your wallet?"

Douglas' eyes darted up from his dinner to meet mine for the first time that night. "What are you talking about?" he said very carefully, as if I was a rabid dog.

"I looked in your wallet, so sue me, and I found that dainty little envelope with Tony the Tiger and Jumbo the Elephant inside. What the hell are you doing with that bill? If you're planning on leaving me and jetting off to India, I think you'll need a few more rupees than that."

Douglas slowly put down his fork, wiped his mouth, placed his napkin on the table and stood up. He started to walk from the kitchen, leaving me sitting there like an idiot. But then he turned and looked straight at me.

"We are as different as dollar and rupee, as tiger and elephant. You would eat me alive if you could, but I won't let you. Unlike you, I know who I am. Unlike you, I have aspirations. And unlike you, I am leaving. You can keep the rupee note as a memento of our marriage."

And that was it. I guess I got a little greedy, and Douglas won the damn game. Now what am I supposed to do with myself?

Going Commercial

Andrei Konchalovsky
translation: Bryon McWilliams

I shot my first TV commercial in France, a coffee ad that was stylish and successful, even won awards. Thanks to commercials I met many beautiful, and very beautiful, women. Most importantly, though – for me, as a director – I met first-class cameramen.

The best cinematographers in the world work in commercials. I met Pasqualino De Santis, who had worked with Zeffirelli, Visconti, and Bresson. I met Tonino Delli Colli, who shot *The Gospel According to St. Matthew* and *Once Upon a Time in America*. I also met Ennio Guarnieri, whom I consider a genius — and with whom I later made the film *The Inner Circle*.

Commercials demand a tremendous concentration of imagery. Self-expression is at a minimum. The only criterion is satisfying the client looking over your shoulder at each and every frame. Each frame needs to make the client happy. It's an elementary philosophy: You like it? Good. You don't like it? Tell me what you want, and we'll redo it.

Nevertheless, commercials made for interesting work. (Of course I didn't make them with the same professional brilliance as, say, Ridley Scott; he gained his reputation through commercials.) Plus they paid a lot.

When they sent me the money for my first commercial I went bonkers. I decided that I could afford pretty much anything, and, in keeping with my former Soviet habits, truly let loose. I began to fly first-class. I stayed in the best hotels, surrounded by fashion models.

You show up for three days of shooting, and two days of preparation, and you leave with $100,000 in your pocket. As the work keeps rolling in, it seems as if you've already earned enough to provide for your own burial. Life seems easy, affordable, and that's the most dangerous thing: no one is allowed to rest on his laurels.

I believed in my own success, but it turned out to be an illusion, a sublime deception. And, oh, how that deception ripped the rug out from under me!

As soon as I began to relax, the quality of my work dropped off, and my reputation came crashing down. My connections with producers were severed.

In commercials one day you're in, and the next day you're out. Everyone is replaceable. Behind you stretches a long line of hungry young directors, and their work is no worse than yours.

Happiness can't be found in money, but in the fact that one has money.

I would re-learn this truth numerous times.

Sons and Silkworms

Christine Johnson

Mei Si sat in a sunny spot, finishing a piece of cloth on the loom. The task was labour following a set pattern. Her slim fingers plied their quiet work, manipulating silken threads with nimble precision. Her insatiable thoughts danced free, weaving their own design. There was little opportunity to reflect at this, the most productive time of the year. Daughter-in-law and now mother of two young boys, it was rare Mei Si's mind could ever wander far from home.

She smiled, recalling her fear as the bridal sedan chair carried her to this place. Matchmakers had bargained down to the bottom line, completed arrangements between the two families, settling on agreed terms. Her parents had brought Mei Si up to understand her fate. She could never marry a man without being traded into his family. Her smile faded as her hungry imagination wondered where her husband Chun was now.

Putting fear aside she glanced instead towards the children, listened for the reassuring sound of their breathing. First son Fen Fei and second boy Hoi Wong, born seven months after his father's departure for the New Gold Mountain. Both slept. Mother and sons, all three enmeshed in the delicate lines of unseen forces as if wrapped in weightless threads of silk.

Time and exacting Mother-in-law had schooled Mei Si. Once married, restraint must rule.

"Wives must forget the self-indulgent spontaneity of girlhood," the older woman warned.

Mei Si sighed. If she knew one thing by now, it was how much of a woman's life Time consumed in waiting.

At least bearing a first boy earned her respect. The pride on her husband's face! The birth saved him from the greatest of the three unfilial acts: leaving no descendants.

"My son will continue the family line," he said, lifting the infant she held out to him. "In time bear the responsibilities of worshipping the ancestors."

As a wife, Mei Si had watched her body swell and produce the required result. Fathers, sons, grandsons in succession, fuelled the cult-of-care, kept the spirits of the dead happy.

And despite Chun's absence, her second child's arrival too had passed with all proper celebration. Of course Mother-in-law prayed eagerly for another grandson. Satisfied, she was generous for once towards her daughter-in-law, bountiful with praise.

"This second son is a true gift," she said. "He is a fine piece of jade with which the gods intend to summon my own son speedily home."

Despite the buoyant words, it was clear to Mei Si this ageing woman struggled with a deeper sadness. Time was passing. As the first months of this second child's life came and went, Mother-in-law secretly despaired. Speaking to the gods her voice became feeble.

"Surely my son should have returned by now?"

Anxiety led her to concentrate fondest attention back onto the firstborn grandchild. Mei Si knew looking at this boy, his Grandmother detected glimpses of his father in him. But, memory fading, only his father remembered as a child.

Mei Si's mind kept active, resisting all hints of misery. Optimistically she looked at Chun's sons, seeing them shining, calling him back. She believed they were something he would in time take pride in and value.

An ancient fortune-teller she visited as a girl had beamed, leaning towards her and nodding.

"I see marriage, many, many sons and a long, fortunate life with your husband," the fortune-teller predicted.

That promise was alive in Mei Si still. Watching over her sons, she heard thoughts about Chun most clearly. Perseverance provided consolation. While it lived, she could wait patiently. She put aside doubts and all questioning of what her husband was doing, replacing them with plans for a time when she would welcome him home.

Meanwhile she was not idle. All around, young pigs to be seen to, setting hens to watch, grain and roots to be sorted, washing and mending to be done, food to be prepared. Her work seemed never-ending.

Even the small silkworms, Mei Si thought not for the first time – what a nuisance they could be for a busy human keeper at this early stage of their development! Such greed! Consuming fresh mulberry leaves, bunches and bunches of them at a startling rate; nothing but insatiable, wriggling dynamos of appetite.

But then Mei Si relented. She thought ahead to when, no longer ravenous and restless, these tiny beings would begin to diligently spin their own pale shrouds. When this time approached she knew, as always, she would observe them with interest. Hold them curiously up to the light one by one, inspecting their miniature, almost-transparent bodies. And finally, she would have the satisfaction of gathering the fruits of their efforts.

Boiling them alive, dipping the cocoons in the steaming water until soft, she would take her needle and painstakingly prick the thread loose. Slowly, carefully, she would unwind the lengthy, yielding strand. Later, homemade dyes would stand ready to accept the threads, turning them into the stuff for her future embroidery and weaving. From the feeding insatiable silkworms and the moths they grew into in their silver-white cocoons, glowing fabrics and exquisitely stitched images would emerge.

Today's work on the loom finished, Mei Si stretched, casting a last look at the silkworms. She realised, in an odd way they, like her sons, meant contentment, keeping her company as she waited: linked her to reality, further labour and her belief in that hopeful future still to come.

Thinking about it, she couldn't imagine life without them.

The Recent History of the Sánchez Family Tragedies: Part III

Guilie Castillo Oriard

Anselmo grew up knowing he was different. He looked different from his sisters, even from his brother. Not enough that people noticed, but *he* did. Everyone else had brown eyes, like The Doctor, or green, like Maura; only he had blue. He was the oldest (eight years between him and Inés, the next closest), but there was no privilege in it. Toño, the youngest, always sat up front in the car with Mama and The Doctor; Anselmo had to squeeze into the back seat with the girls. At seven, Toño was charged with saying grace at family dinners; Anselmo was never allowed, not while The Doctor lived in that house. Toño was taught—shooting, carpentry, math, football—with what amounted to patience, even pride; Anselmo, always top of his class and good with his hands, had never been able to ask The Doctor for help without being called stupid, clumsy, useless in every way.

No one got the beatings he did (except Maura). Even Toño usually got only the belt, maybe a punch or two if the transgression was serious. (Like the day when Toño, a wide-eyed little boy who took everything seriously, who was easily hurt, set the spiral staircase to the roof on fire. For that incident, Anselmo got a dislocated shoulder, a concussion, and a broken rib. Toño received his first punch. Just one, straight across the cheek. Anselmo was eighteen. Toño was just six.)

The greatest difference, though, had to do with his mother. Maura was devoted to all her children, but it wasn't a secret that she saved her best, most lavish love, for her oldest. They sat together in the kitchen every morning, before the household woke, and giggled quietly into cups of very milky coffee or spoke in hushed but hopeful tones about Anselmo's future. That was, by far, their favorite subject.

The other children sometimes complained: why did she love Anselmo more? She couldn't explain to them—about the German boy with the blue eyes Anselmo had inherited, about her overriding need to give him a father, about her guilt and even complicity in the abuse he received (she had married The Doctor, hadn't she?), about the sleepless nights in the grip of regret so powerful it left her weak and disoriented—so instead she scoffed, made excuses, pleading in subtext that they might understand what she couldn't put into words: "He's not like you. He looks strong, but he's not. And he suffers so much. He needs me."

I've often wondered how much Anselmo knew about his paternity. He was eight when Maura married The Doctor; old enough to remember the fatherless years. Your father argues, still today, he cannot have known, and I understand why he chooses to believe that—acknowledging his own father lied to him every single day of his life must be hard—but I disagree. I was closest to Maura of all her grandchildren, maybe the whole family (except Anselmo himself). He was so smart, your grandfather—so *bright!* He would've guessed. Maybe she didn't tell him everything, only enough so he'd know he was a child of love (not, as The Doctor insisted when drunk, of lust and sin).

Anselmo, as early as his twelfth year, knew for a fact he had no blood ties to the man he called Father. I believe that's what kept him sane (saner?). Because, around the time Maura was pregnant with Toño, Anselmo was sent to Maura's parents. Perhaps it was a difficult pregnancy; perhaps Anselmo had been causing trouble (those were his most rebellious years). In any case, the ten months at the Haleys' did what The Doctor's 'discipline' hadn't: he returned reformed, responsible, almost adult.

He had found the documents.

The adoption papers, first, but those weren't as damning. Then the transactions, dated the day of the wedding. He remembered that day. He had been made to wear long pants for the first time, a suit of grey flannel, to walk down the aisle in front of his mother. (Not a church aisle; a civil registrar of some sort.) At the small reception afterwards, he'd barged in on a scene he would've forgotten until the day he saw the documents: Papa Haley in his study with Mama's new husband, writing on some long, boring-looking papers. Papa Haley shooed him out, more gently than he deserved, he remembered thinking.

Papa Haley had paid The Doctor. Bought him, essentially, as a husband for his daughter, a father for his grandchild, and respectability for the family. The documents showed The Doctor had negotiated ever higher amounts, apparently even threatening, the day of the wedding, to back out if the sum wasn't doubled.

A small payment the day after The Doctor proposed. A lump sum the day of the wedding. Another one the day the adoption became official.

(Too bad Papa Haley hadn't thought to include a preemptive clause, something to turn the money into loans, repayable immediately upon proof of his daughter's, or his grandson's, mistreatment.)

In the debris left by the tornado of shock, Anselmo discovered three things. First, relief: he wasn't related to the greedy, grubby-fingered Doctor. Second, a sense of empathy, much too profound for a twelve-year-old, toward his mother: she and he were hostages, fellow prisoners sold as chattel. Their camaraderie, now given new context, would only deepen and grow.

The third discovery unsettled him a little. Mixed in with the lazy love he'd always felt for his siblings (half-siblings; he'd have to get used to that), he now found a weird sort of condescending pity. They were byproducts of greed, of violence. Not their fault; they couldn't help it.

Neither could he.

*   *   *

When he came home, Maura was in bed with the new baby. "His name is José Antonio, Toño for short. What do you think? Want to hold him?"

Anselmo could not.

Jeb, Earl and the Gopher

Steven Carr

Sitting on the back steps of his ramshackle house, Earl quickly raised his rifle and shot at the gopher that stuck its head out of the ground. The bullet missed the gopher, who had ducked back down in the ground and shot off the scraggly leaves of a carrot in the poorly tended vegetable garden. Jeb lowered the rifle and spat out a mouthful of soupy brown chewing tobacco, some of which dribbled down his stubbled chin. He laid the rifle across his lap and wiped the tobacco from his chin with the back of his hand.

Jeb, Earl's older brother, opened the torn screen door and stepped out holding a manilla envelope. "Ya shootin' at that varmint again?" he said.

"Yep, it's dang near eaten all the turnips and beets and was startin' in on the carrots," Earl said.

Jeb sat down on the step next to his brother. "That gopher's one greedy little critter. He done ate half the garden."

"Yep," Earl said, and then spat out some tobacco juice.

Jeb opened the envelope and took out several sheets of paper stapled together. He slowly flipped through them.

"What ya got there?" Earl said.

Jeb read the last sheet. "Darn if Uncle Clarence over in Piney Creek ain't gone and died and left me twenty thousand dollars. This is what they call a will and all I got to do is take these here papers to the courthouse and then the bank and I can collect the money."

Earl rubbed a smudge of dirt from the barrel of his rifle. "Why'd Uncle Clarence just leave his money to you?"

Jeb stood up. "Well, these here papers says he left the money to his next of kin. We're his only next of kin so I figure I got more right to the money than you do."

"How do you figure that?"

"I'm the oldest, the smartest, and I can think of more ways to spend twenty thousand dollars."

Earl spit out the wad of tobacco that had been tucked into his cheek. It landed in the dirt like a turd dropped by a flying pig. "Them papers you got don't say anythin' about any of that, do they? You're just like that greedy sonabitch gopher."

Jeb opened the screen door. "I'll soon be a gopher with twenty thousand dollars." The door closed behind him.

Earl raised his gun and shot at the gopher who was pulling a carrot into a hole. The bullet missed. The gopher and the carrot disappeared into the ground.

* * *

Jeb was sound asleep on the raggedy sofa with the will lying on his stomach. A half empty jug of moonshine sat on the floor next to him. Flies buzzed around his food-caked whiskers.

Earl entered the room planning on demanding Jeb give him half of the money, but seeing his brother in an inebriated state, he took the will and walked out the back door of the house. In the darkness of night, the toads from the nearby pond were croaking and an owl in a nearby tree hooted.

I'll take this here will-thing to the bank in the morning myself, he thought. *I deserve that money more than Jeb does.*

He walked through the garden looking for holes dug by the gopher. When he found one near a patch of cucumbers that had been half eaten by the gopher, he shoved the will into the hole.

* * *

When Henry the rooster let out his usual crowing at the break of dawn, Jeb woke up, swatted away a fly that was sitting on his nose, and sat up. He licked his parched lips and then remembered the will. After ripping apart the sofa and strewing its torn cushions around the room and overturning the rest of the rickety furniture, he took his shotgun down from the rack on the wall and stormed into Earl's bedroom. Earl was fast asleep and snoring loudly, brown spittle on the corners of his mouth.

With the barrel of the gun an inch away from Earl's nose, Jeb said, "Get up you low down good-for-nothing snake in the grass."

Earl awoke with a start. Wide-eyed he stared up the length of the gun. "You gone crazy?" he said as he pushed the gun away from his face. He sat up and shoved Hoss, his hound dog, off the bed.

"You got my will and I want it back," Jeb said, aiming the gun at Earl's chest.

"It ain't yer will. I got as much right to that money as you."

Jeb raised the barrel of the gun and aimed it at Earl's head. "Get me my will or I'll blow yer head off."

Earl climbed out of bed and put on his jeans. "It's out in the garden." He walked out of the bedroom and out of the house.

Jeb followed, holding his gun aimed at Earl's back.

When Earl reached the hole where he had hidden the will, he stared into an empty space.

"Dang nabbit, I think that sonabitch gopher got the will," he said.

Jeb lowered his gun and stared into the hole. "You sure this is the right hole?"

"Yep, it's the hole alright. That greedy gopher will take anythin' it can get its grubby little paws on. Who knows how deep down in its tunnels it's taken the will. It could take years to find it."

Jeb aimed the gun at his brother. "Get the shovel and start diggin'."

Gunfight at the Shopping-Cart Corral

Alan C. Baird

So, the wife and I were shopping at our local natural-foods grocery store this morning. No, we're not tree-huggers. They just have a nice fruit section. Peaches and shit.

We were browsing through the peach aisle when my wife urgently pulled me aside: "Did you see that guy?"

"What guy?" I craned my neck to peek around behind her.

"Don't look. He might shoot."

"Whaaaat?!" That really captured my attention. Sure enough, some corpulent 80-year-old asshole was standing in front of the donut peaches, packing a pistol. Rosewood-checkered grip, tooled-leather holster, the whole bit. Not a law enforcement guy, just some retired jerkoff who evidently wanted to enhance the perceived size of his schlong.

Allow me to digress for a moment: the last time I wore a gun and a tooled-leather holster, I was six years old. I had imaginary shootouts with Tommy, who lived next door. Our guns were just cap pistols. Nobody got hurt, unless you tried to drop a big rock on several rolls of caps. (Don't try this at home. I speak from experience.) We loved wearing the full cowboy drag. And we enjoyed using our guns and holsters.

Until we outgrew them.

At age seven.

I mean, everybody outgrows them, right?

Well, apparently not.

Okay, back to Mister Second-Fucking-Amendment: when I saw that gun in the grocery store, steam started shooting from my ears. I marched up to the front office and loudly demanded to see the manager. When he arrived, I was apoplectic: "If you're gonna allow this kind of behavior in your store, I'm not gonna shop here anymore."

The manager was apologetic: "I can't stop him. Arizona is an Open-Carry state."

"You can't post a 'No Firearms Allowed' sign on the door?"

"Sadly, no."

I riposted: "Bars can do it."

"I know. But that's because they sell alcohol."

"Then it's high time to get a liquor license."

He nodded. "I hear you."

"So, guns are off-limits in bars, schools, government buildings, airports and airliners. You think it's a good idea to allow them in your grocery store?"

"No, but..."

"And it's not like this white-bread neighborhood is dangerous. The worst criminals you have are jaywalkers."

"Exactly. I recently moved here from California, and I can't believe what these people get away with."

I pulled out the big guns: "Displaying a gun is an implied threat of violence. His threat has spread fear in your customers. Instilling fear is a hallmark of terrorism. Under some definitions, he has already committed a terrorist act."

He sympathized. "Guns are just murders waiting to happen." But then he shrugged.

The shrug derailed me. What's that Edmund Burke quote? "All that is necessary for evil to triumph is for good people to do nothing."

I shuffled back to the peach aisle, tail between my legs. The gun-totin' asshole had moved over to the nectarine aisle. My wife said: "Well?"

"It's legal. Nothing to be done."

"You're kidding." Let me explain: she's European. And like most civilized people, she often has trouble understanding some of Arizona's medieval laws.

I shook my head. "Nope. And I can't say anything to him. If he's psycho enough to wear a gun in a grocery store, he's psycho enough to use it. All of us would end up on the evening news, looking like Swiss cheese."

She was silent for a long time. "You're afraid of him?"

"Duh."

"Then I will buy you a gun at Christmas. And you will buy one for me."

"Huh?" I couldn't believe my ears. Every now and then, she has trouble with the English language. I was beginning to wonder if this was one of those times.

"We will return here on December 26th, and we will stand in front of that old fasz with our brand-new guns, and we will call him out." 'Fasz' is the Hungarian word for 'prick.' When she starts peppering her conversation with Magyar expletives, it's a pretty good indication she's having no trouble at all with her English. "And if he tries to walk away, we will laugh at the size of his tiny shriveled-up fasz."

"He'll draw. You know he'll draw."

"He's old. We're faster."

The Return of Red Ledbetter
Episode 3: All That Glitters

JP Lundstrom

"Now, Detective—what can I do for you?" Matabang Lalaki waited.

Detective Red Ledbetter observed Lalaki. The glutton had devoured fifteen courses, and not one crumb was offered the detective.

"I'd like to speak with your delivery man."

"I have several."

The dead man in the alley waited. The murdered woman in apartment 810 had all eternity. And though it was Christmas Eve, Ledbetter had no other plans, no family waiting at home. His holiday would be spent working. Let the greedy bastard wait.

He surveyed the opulent décor. "Nice."

Lalaki chuckled. "My apartment upstairs is decorated similarly."

Red scratched his head. "Must cost a pretty penny."

"It's not about the money. The important thing is living well."

"Still, the cost…" Lalaki's income could stand a closer look.

"Oh, make no mistake—one must have money. Fortunately, that's not a problem."

"Oh, really? Your family?"

The fat man snorted. "Hardly. My parents were peasants, uneducated and unmotivated. Their lives were spent in muck and mire, struggling to keep food in their mouths. That was my heritage, and I despised it."

"A harsh Christmas Eve sentiment."

"What they lacked in ambition, I made up for in an avid desire to better myself. You're looking at a self-made man."

"And your parents?"

"Dead and buried."

"But you helped them while they were alive?"

"Why should I? They gave me nothing."

"They gave you life."

"What they gave me could by no stretch of the imagination be called life. It was pure torture for a sensitive youth. I was meant for better things."

"Such as…?"

"I was attracted to beauty—a painting, a sculpture, even the regular features and well-formed physique of an attractive person. I became an educated man."

"A scholar—that seems a worthy aspiration."

Lalaki gave a sweep of his hand. "I wanted more—recognition, influence, beauty, and of course, money."

"Of course."

"Rest assured, all my enterprises are quite legal—this restaurant, for example. I own the building, too, among others."

Ledbetter glanced around again. "Good for you."

"I collect beautiful things." Heavy chins rested on steepled hands.

"Still working—on Christmas Eve?" A woman entered, carrying a gift-wrapped package. The woman from the elevator.

Lalaki continued. "A man has longings, desires…"

Needs… Ledbetter watched the sway of her hips.

She spoke. "A gift from *Grand-mère*."

"Thank you, my dear." He accepted the package, placing it on the table. "Detective Ledbetter, may I present Miss Belle Charmant?"

"My pleasure." Ledbetter grinned.

"Detective." She turned to Lalaki. "Aren't you going to open it?"

"Presently. May I offer you a drink? A very nice *baijiu* with a lovely fragrance." Lalaki's eyes roamed over her. He raised his glass. "Sniff."

She leaned forward, then coughed. "Oh! It's very strong, isn't it?"

Lalaki chuckled. "Shall I pour you a glass?"

"I'd better be going." She buttoned her coat, pulled on her gloves. *"Joyeux Noël."*

"Merry Christmas. Regards to your grandmother."

Both men gazed after her.

"As I was saying, I appreciate the finer things." Lalaki's pudgy hand fluttered through his hair. "I know what I want, and I pursue it until it is mine."

Ledbetter didn't have time for this. "Mr. Lalaki, I just want to speak with your delivery boy, the one with the tattoos."

"Ah—you mean Tagata Pe'a!" Lalaki smoothed his red silk tie. An inexperienced cop might not have noticed the twitch in his left eye. "A Samoan boy. He's an excellent courier."

"He delivers food?"

"Among other things."

"For example?"

"He does whatever I tell him." Lalaki had lost patience, too.

* * *

"Where is he?" The woman burst into the room, her flaming red hair wild, the clothing on her tiny frame in disarray. Chichu followed.

She grabbed at the intruder. "I tried to keep her out."

"Hands off, Spider!" The redhead shrugged out of her grasp.

Lalaki breathed the sigh of the long-suffering. "Detective, meet Fiamma Pericolosa, also known as Mrs. Peter Dick."

The dead man's wife!

Lalaki continued, "She used to work for me, but now..."

So she no longer kowtowed to Lalaki's whims, and he was sensitive about it.

"I asked you a question." The little redhead confronted her former boss.

Lalaki's hands lifted in mock surrender. "The fact that your husband enjoys dining in the Golden Dragon doesn't enable me to know his whereabouts twenty-four hours a day. I assume he's a healthy, active man with an interesting and varied social life. I suggest you may find your answer with any one of a number of young ladies all over the city."

Her hands became fists at her sides. "You—slug!"

"If there's nothing else, I'll have Chichu call you a cab."

"Don't bother."

Ledbetter followed the angry woman. "Mrs. Dick!"

She stopped. "Who are you?"

He gave her his card.

"You're with the police?"

"Yes, ma'am."

"You know something about my husband?"

"May I speak with you later? I know it's Christmas, but—"

Sliding her own card from a fancy silver case, she placed it in his hand. "Here's the address."

Manor Oaks, as the dead woman had said. The redhead was in for an unpleasant Christmas surprise.

Ledbetter finished with Lalaki and returned to his partner, and the building where it all began.

Fiamma, Chichu, Luz, even Belle—were they part of his collection?

Lalaki was as stuck in his greed as his parents had been in poverty, always wanting more, never satisfied. Greed, in the end, is a lonely road.

There are three things that rule the world: stupidity, fear, and greed. Lalaki had accomplished two.

The ride up to the eighth floor was cold and solitary. When the elevator doors opened, he heard gunfire.

"It came from 808!" Wilson was already attacking the door. A final kick, and it flew open.

Ledbetter stepped in, gun raised. "Police!"

Standing over a man's body, a pistol in her trembling hands, was Belle Charmant.

"I didn't do it!"

Set for Life

Copper Rose

"Well, that's a wrap."

"Yes. Poor fellow. He died so quickly he never got to sign his will," Maude called from the lobby where she turned the closed sign in the bank window. She hurried back to Terrence's office.

"His money's going to the school, which is appropriate, doing something nice for the kids since we all knew Gordon couldn't read or write." Terrence peered at his secretary over the top of his glasses. "At least everyone thinks it will all go to the school."

A smile spread across Maude's face. "There are rumors rolling about town his father did it on purpose, kept Gordon from reading and writing, never let him look at books."

"It didn't help that his mother died when she fell down a well just after he was born. So, ah, did you take care of the original copy of his will?"

"Yes, I did." Maude didn't miss a beat. "I heard his father was a womanizer. With parents like that, Gordon never had a chance."

"Lucky for us he wasn't poor. His father's womanizing paid off. The old man must have had quite the charismatic personality to swindle all those widows out of their fortunes. Being an only child, Gordon was set for life." Terrence rubbed his hands together. "He had no living relatives and he didn't trust anyone. Bill Barker, the barber, told me he suspected Gordon was rich, but no one knows how much money Gordon really had."

"Even Gordon never knew because of his inability to read."

"Yes, that was his tragedy."

"He may have had some idea how much was in his account; but he wasn't able to manage it effectively because he couldn't read the bank statements. The receptionist here told me Gordon could write some numbers, although not very well and if he tried really hard, he was able to write his name."

"Yes, I heard he kept lists of phone numbers written on the lids of shoeboxes."

"Yes, I saw his lists. With all those shoes did he think he was going somewhere?"

"Well he's gone now. Lucky for us." Terrence lifted a stack of papers into his briefcase and snapped it closed. "Say, what was the name of that woman he kept asking to marry him?"

"Adrienne. She said no to him while he was on his death bed. She applied for a loan here, but the loan manager had to turn her down."

"Pity. I heard her husband died and left her penniless. Such a shame after all those years she stuck by him. What's she doing for money?"

"No one knows. She's one of those eccentric ones who can stretch a dime until it looks like two nickels."

"Another tragedy. She should have said yes to Gordon. If she would have married him *she* would have been set for life," Terrence said as he winked at Maude.

"I heard that after Adrienne's husband died she vowed never to marry again. It's her loss." Maude stuffed a file in the cabinet and slammed the drawer shut with a bump from her hip as Terrence snatched up his briefcase.

Terrence stepped through the door and headed down the hall, with thoughts of Bermuda dancing in his head.

Maude grabbed her purse and then noticed a red folder on her desk. She scooped it up and hurried after Terrence. "Darling, you forgot your folder."

Terrence stopped midstride and twisted to face Maude. "That's not my folder."

"I must have missed it when I was filing Gordon's papers. It must be his."

"What in the world — what could be in it? This account is supposed to be closed."

They hurried back into the office. Maude threw the file on the desk and yanked open the folder. They stared at the sheet of paper inside. Across the top was Gordon's chicken-scratch signature, along with a date that looked as though a child had scribbled it under his name. Below that was a picture of a house, drawn with a black magic marker – and what appeared to be a safe inside the house, a vault, with a turn dial. Below that was an arrow pointing to a number.

"Oh dear, I think this is Gordon's version of a final will. And he signed it. If that really is Gordon's signature then it's binding."

Terrence ripped the paper from Maude's hands. "What? There's no name listed here about where his money should go, like the copy we have on file listing the school, and his, uh, adjusted assets — just, just a signature and a number. And some pitiful drawings. Pictures aren't binding –"

Maude pulled a shoebox lid from the file cabinet. "The arrow is pointing to what looks like a phone number – and it matches the number on this shoebox lid. Somebody's going to get everything Gordon has…but…but that's not a problem. We'll just destroy this copy."

Terrence peered over Maude's shoulder and pointed to the word COPY. "This isn't the original."

Maude and Terrence stared at each other and then Maude's hand trembled as she reached for the phone. Terrence glared over the top of his glasses as Maude dialed the number on the sheet. Maude hit the button to activate the speaker phone. They leaned in and listened as the phone rang three times before someone picked up.

"Hello, this is Adrienne Wolski. How can I help you?"

Sunday

Edward Reilly

It's one thing to be a damned good teacher, good technically and, or even good morally, the two do not necessarily go together, be top of the tree and all that, but it's another not to have a school. Such a situation is nothing short of a total disaster for someone whose life, from those first words uttered on his mother's knee whilst she was tutoring a neighbour's bairn in the use of *voudrais*, to his first practice round at the old Geelong Technical School in a draughty, unheated portable plonked next to the automobile machine shop, then to last Term's revision seminars he'd run for the local Catholic schools' mathematics network, had been so enjoyably devoted to his studies and the craft of teaching. He had persisted and had gained some minor notoriety as an advocate of teaching the purest of mathematics to the toughest gang of *tekkies*, before making his escape to holy ground. But now his school, the one in which it was hinted, that languid afternoon before Christmas, they wanted him fast-tracked, but now, this school, this venerable and ancient institution, ancient that is for the bayside of western Melbourne, Altona Catholic Ladies' College, had gone turtle over Christmas, the victim of greed and palace machinations it was said, so he, and sixty other colleagues, bands of disconsolate parents and bewildered kindergarteners had been spilling over onto the road, subject to the fleeting sympathies and snide smiles of their more fortunate secular colleagues.

As he told me at our first meeting, his bank account was empty after Eileen's wedding, silk dress from some snooty sharp-nosed woman who had wanted to colour-coordinate the guests, a reception at Julio's faux-Roman ballroom and overcooked fingerfood, their honeymoon in the Cook Islands. Hopefully, she would return with a tiny bun in the oven and the MacGowans would have an heir, good luck to them all: but Declan was broke. Mind you, Harry Hansen for the Teachers' Solidarity, and some slip of a girl from Catholic Education Office were handing out envelopes marked respectively *We Can Help You* and *Confidential* to the teachers, or else a flyer headed *Transfer Arrangements* to parents. One such, the thickly bearded Mr. Singh, was roaring at Hansen. A few other parents chipped in and were about to give Hansen a good pummelling when the girl, all red hair and spectacles, told them to desist immediately and announced that a parents' meeting would be held over there, pointing to the assembly area: she led the way, waving a clipboard above her head with would-be Kinders clammily clutching onto hands of weepy mothers, stern-faced fathers. Singh and others followed. All Hansen could do was finish handing out the union's letters.

Sr. Rita O'Callaghan, redoubtable head of the Junior School, remarked that she hadn't been told anything about this, and why hadn't she been told?

— After all, I ...

She was interrupted in mid-utterance by Kiernan, the economics teacher, who flipped his head over to the black limousine hovering by the pedestrian crossing.

— Ask himself how much the land's worth for a supermarket!

The crowd of teachers turned towards the car. Hansen called for calm.

— Don't do anything rash! The Monsignor only follows advice given by the Board!

But the pack ignored their chosen representative and moved with murderous intent towards the crouching puma, its engine purring into life.

— He's trying to give us the slip!

Sr. O'Callaghan waved her parasol above the now tightly-bunched group.

— Bloody Hell! You won't get away with this, Morgan!

The driver's blanched face could now be seen through the tinted windshield as he tried to reverse the Jaguar into a nearby cul-de-sac, only to find the exit was blocked by a mass of bewildered seniors, smart in their first-day fresh-pressed finery, bunches of flowers for their beloved teachers now starting to wilt in their hands.

— What's up Sister Rita? Who's in the car?

The girls, with their fierce reputation in Hockey, had begun to sense some good bloodsport. Then it was the turn of Monique Delisle, tall, lithe, the object of every man's lust, resplendent in her tennis whites.

— *C'est le Bête* – she cried out in her best school-teaching accent:

— Bluebeard! *Arrête!*

Her class closed around the sable carriage, entirely stopping its escape. The portly being of Monsignor Morgan Jones sidled out, beaming.

— Why Sr. Marguerite, what's all the fuss about?

But Sr. Rita was having none of this. She stepped up to her cousin-in-law, grabbed one of the girls' flowery offerings and thrust that in his face.

— Take that to His Grace and stick up his, his …

She didn't quite get to finish with an unseemly curse as her blood pressure had begun to play tricks again and collapsed at his feet, her hem lifting up just above knees to expose pale flesh rising out of her black half-stockings. Delisle hastily rearranged her superior's dress and had some of her girls raise the stricken nun to a sitting position. But Jones was unmoved.

— Get up, you silly cow!

He muttered loudly enough for the girls to hear and exhale a collective *O!*

— We've had enough of your histrionics for today!

Mgr. Jones, more loudly this time, jutted out his jaw at Hansen.

— It's her party trick: every Christmas, any funeral. It's the same!

Declan had gone to the women's aid, helping them to a shaded area. The remaining teachers and senior students bunched tightly around the lonely black figure of the Monsignor like a herd of wild cattle staring down a guilty fox. But such is the power of the collar that he was able to ease himself back into the limousine, and the crowd parted like the waters of the Red Sea as his car purred away.

The Promise

Abha Iyengar

Sidhartha was celebrating his seventy-eighth birthday. He had lived a long and fruitful life, working at the head of the company he owned, and still did. His relatives had been telling him to pass on the reins to his only son, Yaman, born from his first wife, Sarita, now dead for the last twenty years. Yaman, was fifty, not young by any chance. His only grandchild, Surin, was thirteen. "The only child of an only child," sighed Sidhartha, "but how young and handsome is this fruit from my son's loins." He chuckled to himself and rubbed his hands with glee.

No one understood why Sidhartha held on to the reins of his empire, and why his son still played second fiddle to him. And he was not telling anyone. He was waiting for his seventy-eighth birthday to pass. Then, he would take his grandson on a promised holiday, a trip to an island. He had prepared everything.

The doctor was ready. He would do all that was required to transfer his grandson's youth to him through blood transfusions. This doctor was only known to a few, and he had performed wonders on a handful of old, wealthy people. It was essential that there be a young family member whose youth could be sacrificed. There would be nothing left of Surin once this was over, but Sidhartha could deal with that, because of the promise that he would emerge younger and more agile than even his own son. That was what the doctor had promised in return for an unmentionable fee. He could then continue to reign over his family and company for another three decades.

The examples the doctor had shown had convinced Sidhartha. He had just transferred the half a billion dollars to the doctor's account. He looked at his face every day in the mirror and did not recognize himself. He loathed what he saw, a bag of sagging wrinkles, a man with rheumy eyes and a bent body. "Youth," he toasted, his toothy face breaking into a smile, "here's to youth!"

As he envisioned himself as a young man, he keeled over. The noise of the falling body and chair made people rush in, and Yaman and Surin found Sidhartha prone on the floor, his face wreathed in a smile.

Surin clung to the dead body. "I'll miss you, Grandpa," he sobbed.

Gaslighter in the Morgue – Touching Up Beauty

Alison Fish

When you own a morgue, you repair the irreparable. Every household hides secrets, ours enshrouds evil. The townsfolk branded us the Addams Family. We, the Sindons, had garnered respect for dealing with death across generations. On the outside, we were transparent. Informally, we counselled the newly bereaved. We gave out cards for healing, talk therapy and even clairvoyance. We supported believers whose fears of sinful transgression were weaker than their loneliness or curiosity. We provided a menu of funeral styles, coffins and condolence paraphernalia: flowers, poems, blessings. Ours was a comprehensive service for the broken souls left breathing. For the guilty, the parish priest held weekly confessionals, guaranteeing anonymity. He knew how secrets stink.

The guardian of my own Pandora's Box was Uncle Ricky-Rezo Sindon, Chief Undertaker, my father's older brother, "el lobo poderoso". Ricky-Rezo was my godfather, embalmer and our household "wolf". He fitted the role of Lurch: wily eyes, nose for a scent and friendly until provoked. In situations requiring empathy, I took the professional helm, quietly shifting him sideways, blocking his conversations with a sturdy box of tissues and a sharp elbow. Weeping customers turned his knuckles white. He struggled to restrain his demons, hiding a rainbow-beast of a temper that would make Cerberus flinch. He didn't "do" emotion, yet his salacious laughter pursued me throughout childhood.

Before puberty, I'd spoken out. Our priest blanched and I was labelled an unreliable narrator. My family, the jury, led by my uncle Ricky, the perpetrator, had treated me as a clown, a Pierrot, blushing with insecurities. Every insinuation was skilfully diffused without drama. Eventually I stayed quiet. Uncle Ricky's intimidation sliced through my ego. The fearful bludgeon of cunning eyes kept me in check. Feeling belittled was enough to force my head down; unsavoury shenanigans. My aunt's silent pity was denial. Gazing at me, the tendons in her neck twitched tight. A wife knows. Later, as a teenager, I imagined being accused of perjury. I was immune to feeling stripped of my dignity. There was no self-defence, no ally. No-one believed me. I just got on. Hardly a joy ride when someone else's cabaret never stops.

Growing up, my peers were wary. Embracing the role of six-toed Wednesday, I learned to glower and scare the pants off the playground teasers. A few loyal classmates accepted invitations for the best Hallowe'en makeovers. Here my face-paints were used in reverse. Instead of a healthy pink oyster glow, my palette of icy blues and mauves was fundamental, adding scars instead of camouflaging defects. Art was my talent and following my family's vocation was undisputed. In hindsight, I might have run away to an apprenticeship in a "cheeky" tattoo parlour. But business is business.

In the beginning, Ricky-Rezo the wolf and I were a winning team. But as I grew into womanhood, I was bullied into cruel submission. To hide the hierarchy, #the-puppy-of-the-pack, #themortuarybeautician, I was always fully made-up. Schoolmates begged for teenage transformations. I spent hours practising skills as a cosmetologist. My bristled wand hid bruises and camouflaged tears. I created the bare-faced look, but post-punk art was my ace-card, focussing on chiselled cheeks, candy-rouge and stiff hair-gels. My magic mirror reflected awesome beauty. The complete mannequin effect was a perfect plastic Barbi or Siouxsie-Sioux – Dying to be beautiful, is she or isn't she? Dead or alive?

Uncle Ricky would reach a familiar finger to my fashioned face demanding a touch-up: a greater arch of brow or extensions to the hair I'd braided. The finished look was worth the cheque. Customers marvelled at how I transformed lifelessness. Funny how quickly I would become a spinster-battleaxe, a "Grandma Frump" with a low curl to my own mouth. Thanks to my uncle's physical blows.

Uncle Ricky organised outfits, suits and twin-sets. The shocked and grieving were inept at choosing the final accoutrement for their deceased. Every corpse was measured precisely. Upsized shoes cost extra because feet swell. I never suspected that my own measurements were on his mind.

After my widowed father's sudden death, our family business was mine by inheritance. Ricky was next in line. In those days despite his lewdness, he had my trust. How naïve I was and hypnotically oblivious to his plotting, his envy, his insatiable greed. Over time, family pride and anti-depressants had made me compliant, obedient to his heinous wolfish advances.

When father died, the Wolf had two coffins ready. The penny didn't drop. We had always laughed over beers, describing our preferred funeral number. Dad's was the George Formby ukulele tune waiting for his "Certain Little Lady". He imagined meeting my mother at the pearly gates. We often updated our choice of songs, though none of us had written a testament.

At first I retched. Painstakingly, my nimble strokes gave Father's blue pallor a delicate yellowish glow, until his face was perfect. Ricky tailored all the suits to cater for ballooning, the natural result of a body's decay. My father's glassy-eyed sadness disguised with pearl plush was the last thing I'd see. Stooping at his temples, my uncle's quiet shadow went undetected. I was caught off-guard by a blow to the head. Blacking out, I lost consciousness. I don't know when I caught my last breath.

On waking I saw myself from the outside, my own dead body, cosy, tucked-in, plugged and motionless. The casket was the one I'd always preferred, made to measure. Surrounded by comfortable walls of purple satin, my corpse lay stiff. My nails torn, worn from tearing at my prison with my last ounce of energy. I'd spent my lifetime trying to warn the family. Now I watch, floating. With psychic energy I slam doors and seethe at the ironic photograph of myself cross legged on a coffin next to a young Ricky. Forensics will investigate. They may have records. Perhaps there will be a file. My uncle "El Lobo" is destined to pay for his crimes and when his guilty heart stops, who'll be there to make his face pretty?

Greed – Good or Bad?

Jeffrey Weisman

The greedy Gordon Gecko character in the movie *Wall Street* claimed that "greed is good." But for whom?

Greed often fosters the loss of jobs and livelihoods. The executives of Enron allowed greed to destroy their house of cards. Many went to jail.

Greedy and relentless drug dealers ply their never-ending trade; scores of people die or suffer. African animals, elephants and rhinos, die from the greed of poachers.

Corporate greed, particularly now among the large pharmaceutical firms pushing pain pills, has escalated the opiate menace across the country. And the greed of Martin Skrelli pushed him to raise the price of a needed drug by 700%. He's now in jail.

Bernie Madoff made millions of dollars luring gullible investors to his Ponzi scheme. He didn't do it alone; he had help — from those same gullible investors. Greed motivated Madoff and his victims.

Some real estate developers practice an ingenious form of greed. A noted New York City building owner uses a "rubber ruler" in the description of commercial office properties. He'll list an actual 10X12 foot room as 12X14; he adds the space inside the walls to the rental cost.

Greed expresses itself in more subtle ways. Mega-churches amass huge amounts of cash. And while the stated purpose of the ministry is to spread God's word, we rarely know what becomes of all the funds.

"Prosperity Gospel" televangelist Jesse Duplantis from New Orleans, LA recently asked for donations of $54 million to purchase a new Dassault private jet. He claims he can then carry God's word anywhere in the world with only one stop. Another televangelist, Kenneth Copeland from Texas, recently received $36 million for a new Gulfstream.

[Note: At publication we do not know if Duplantis' followers bought him his new plane.]

Greed seems common to the wealthy. I heard a story about a man with a net worth of about $400 million who told of a missed business opportunity to buy shares of Pepsi-Cola in the 1930s. He lamented, "I could have been rich."

Maybe greed has its good side.

The contributions of the Robber Barons of the past resulted in beneficial public installations: Carnegie Hall, Rockefeller Center, Morgan Library, Ford Foundation, etc.

However, we must not forget the human toll that greedy monopolists may have foisted on the public as they accumulated their wealth.

Not all greedy people have mass riches. Some demonstrate a greedy attitude by just pinching their pennies. Should we abide or ignore their selfishness?

What do you think of a person's greed if there's a benefit for you? Might that make you greedy?

Does a greedy business that funds a hospital or a dance company deserve your patronage? What if that greedy business gives nothing back but offers a quality product? How far will you allow greed to enter your life?

So is greed good? I think not. What do you think?

Through a glass, darkly

Rob Walker

Of course I first became aware last night that the piece was missing.

Some might say that I am obsessive. Perhaps they are correct. I am always pleased to share my passion for collecting, but I like to see everything returned to its proper place before retiring. I sent my housekeeper off to bed.

It was then that I realised the Burmese Blue was missing. It is a small piece, my first and I'm particularly fond of it, having acquired it in Rangoon, more than thirty years ago. It was the birth of my interest in the beauty of Burmese glass, and Melodie would have known this, but I'll deal with her later.

I scoured the carpet in my Collection Room, checked behind sofas, lifted cushions and so forth – all to no avail. I was still convinced that it had merely been misplaced, you see. When I found myself repeatedly looking in places I knew I'd checked previously, I became frantic and checked the upstairs rooms. After a sleepless night I determined to notify the Police at a more respectable hour in the morning.

I was up early, busying myself with tidying the house, hard work and routine being something of a comfort for me.

Downstairs, on the duvet in the Guest Room, was a handbag. I couldn't remember whose it was. I opened it and there was Melodie's driver's licence, just loose in the bag. Typical Melodie – she's such a flibbertijibbet, I thought – her

Louis Vuitton had special compartments for licences, but here it was, just thrown in with her lipsticks, compact and nail-file. Then I saw the sparkle of blue.

At that moment it all became clear. My best friend was a thief.

It was as if someone had hit me from behind with a club. I actually reeled forward in shock and had to sit on the bed.

Suddenly I realized I had never really trusted Melodie, with her girlish name and her sing-song voice to match.

We'd had a kind of sororal relationship vacillating between love and hatred. We'd become close at College. She was the party-girl; I was the more reserved. Perhaps she was a little jealous of me. I studied harder and achieved the better grades. It was me, Dorothy Blunt, who steadfastly and persistently built up a portfolio of clients who appreciated my conservative approach to financial management. I'd acquired this substantial home in Adelaide and filled it with beautiful objets d'Art.

Certainly Melodie had the good looks and wasn't averse to flaunting her slim figure at all and sundry.

I've always suspected her of stealing William, my one and only fiancé who just moved to another city one day without having the intestinal fortitude to face me. William and his cowardly two-page letter... Oh, I know he didn't run off with Melodie, but it was she with her loose morals who'd set his eye to straying. Just as she batted those cheap false eyelashes at Neville last night before accepting his lift home. No self-control, Melodie. Can't even steal without making a complete shennanigans. Robs me on impulse, drinks like a dipsomaniac, forgets her bag and allows the first man who asks her to drive her home. I have no doubt Neville had his way with the little strumpet. If she were here now I'd be tempted to bring one of my pieces down on her thin skull, crack! like an almond shell...

However, unlike Melodie Tripp, I have morals. I shall ring the local police and report the theft. Later, in their presence, I shall discover the glass in her ostentatious Louis Vuitton and put on a show of histrionics. She will be met by the full force of the Law.

Melodie may not look quite so pretty in prison garb.

I may even show some Christian charity and visit her in gaol…

Chaos Theory

Michael Webb

I stare at the top of my coffee cup. I had made the cup, fully intending to drink it, but my stomach clutches at the thought of ingesting anything, so I stare. It is quiet, only a blanketing soft bed of normal sounds, the heat coming on, a truck shifting as it accelerates towards the highway. I feel empty, raw and emotional, a way I haven't felt since I was a teen.

I think about a video I watched of a British journalist explaining chaos theory, a close-up of a candle burning, the smoke forming a neat column then exploding into a riot of twisting, disrupted snakes. I was sleepless, my head pounding, the baby finally quiet as the journalist explained about sensitivity to initial conditions, the complex mathematics that explain the way something so simple becomes completely unpredictable.

I see the light of the baby monitor, the green lights that register sound flickering as he changes position or sighs in his sleep. I simultaneously want to race to him, pull him to my chest, and resorb him into my body, as well as get into my car and drive, head west or south to a place where no one has heard of me, where I can sleep and read and sip wine and flirt delicately, become someone without a past. I feel an intense need, almost a mania, a compulsion to snatch him out of the arms of anyone who is holding him, yet the burden of his desires hollows my bones and gnaws at my soul.

I am cemented to my chair with fatigue. I want to sleep, but I am afraid of missing a sniffle or a cry. I can't move, but I have to move. Everything was so simple. Marry, get pregnant, glow with praise and attention, then you have the baby and disappear, feeling torn and sick and miserable, and no one understands the intensity of everything you feel. The coffee cools, and I stare at the lights, and I want to live forever, and I want to run away.

Also from Pure Slush Books

https://pureslush.com/store/

- Gluttony 7 Deadly Sins Vol. 2

ISBN: 978-1-925536-54-6 (paperback) / 978-1-925536-55-3 (eBook)

- Lust 7 Deadly Sins Vol. 1

ISBN: 978-1-925536-47-8 (paperback) / 978-1-925536-48-5 (eBook)

- Happy² Pure Slush Vol. 15

ISBN: 978-1-925536-39-3 (paperback) / 978-1-925536-40-9 (eBook)

- Inane Pure Slush Vol. 14

ISBN: 978-1-925536-17-1 (paperback) / 978-1-925536-18-8 (eBook)

- Freak Pure Slush Vol. 13

ISBN: 978-1-925536-15-7 (paperback) / 978-1-925536-16-4 (eBook)

- Summer Pure Slush Vol. 12

ISBN: 978-1-925536-13-3 (paperback) / 978-1-925536-14-0 (eBook)